SOCCER TEAM UPSET

FRED BOWEN SPORTS STORY series

FRED BOWEN SPORTS STORY *series*

SOCCER TEAM UPSET

PEACHTREE
ATLANTA

Published by
PEACHTREE PUBLISHERS
1700 Chattahoochee Avenue
Atlanta, Georgia 30318-2112
www.peachtree-online.com

Cover design by Thomas Gonzalez and Maureen Withee.
Book design by Melanie McMahon Ives.

Printed and bound in the United States of America
10 9 8 7 6 5 4 3 2 1
First Edition

Library of Congress Cataloging-in-Publication Data
Bowen, Fred.
Soccer team upset / written by Fred Bowen.
p. cm.
Summary: Tyler's hope that his soccer team will be undefeated is dashed when his friend Zack, the team's star midfielder, and two more of the Cougars' best players accept an offer to play for an elite travel team.
ISBN 13: 978-1-56145-495-2 / ISBN 10: 1-56145-495-8
[1. Soccer--Fiction. 2. Teamwork (Sports)--Fiction. 3. Determination (Personality trait)--Fiction.] I. Title.
PZ7.B6724Soc 2009
[Fic]--dc22
2008054866

For Megan—

welcome to the team

Chapter 1

"Back pass!" Tyler Davis called out to his teammate Zack Bell. They had been playing on the same soccer teams since they were little kids. Now they were in seventh grade, playing for the Cougars and battling the Sharks in a scoreless game.

Zack sent the ball spinning right to Tyler's feet. *Zack knows exactly where to pass it,* Tyler thought. He quickly controlled the ball with a foot tap and checked the action on the field. A Sharks defender was charging toward him. Tyler managed to nudge the ball away as his opponent tried to kick it. The defender's foot caught nothing but air and he fell with a thud.

Tyler spotted another teammate, Mario Cruz, racing down the right wing. Tyler set up the ball with a slight tap of his left foot, kicked it with his right, and sent the ball curving downfield.

Mario trapped the ball after one bounce and looked up to see Zack, the Cougars attacking midfielder, angle past a Sharks defender and race to the goal. Mario centered a pass, low and hard, straight to Zack.

The Sharks defense charged toward Zack to block his shot on goal. But it was too late. In a flash Zack rocketed the ball past the goalkeeper.

"Gooooaaaal!" Tyler shouted, stretching the word to the breaking point. *What a shot!* he thought as he raced toward his teammates.

The Cougars crowded around Zack, trading high fives and slapping him on the back.

"Nice pass," Zack said, nodding to Mario.

Mario smiled. "Don't thank me," he said. "Tyler started the play with that pass down the wing."

The Cougars celebration didn't last long. Ms. Murray, their coach, kept them focused on the game. She paced the sidelines, clapping and shouting encouragement as they headed back to their positions. "Good work, guys. Great passes, Tyler and Mario. Don't let up. We're only up by one. Remember to help on defense."

Coach Murray didn't have to worry. The Cougars controlled the rest of the first half, playing with a cool, quiet confidence. Justin Sheridan, the Cougars striker, scored on a header just before the half to increase the Cougars lead to 2–0.

At halftime, the team sprawled on the soft grass under the warm September sunshine and sucked on orange slices.

"Good job, guys," Coach Murray said as she looked around the small circle of players. "I like the passing. Move the ball from side to side. Play possession, like you're playing keep-away. We have a two-goal lead."

"Are we going with the same lineup in the second half?" Tyler asked.

"Tyler's looking to score a goal," Zack whispered to the other Cougars in a teasing voice.

"Same starters for the second half," Coach Murray said, nodding. "I know this is a preseason game, but I want you to play like it's for the championship."

The referee blew his whistle and signaled the teams to get ready.

Coach Murray looked out toward the field. "All right now, let's keep playing hard. Everybody hustle," she said. "We're only up by two goals. The Sharks can come back."

Tyler traded sly smiles with Zack and Mario. *That's what Coach thinks,* he told himself. The Cougars knew they had this game won.

Sure enough, the Cougars controlled the second half, too. From his position on the wing, Tyler watched Zack in awe. His friend kept the ball close to his feet as he dodged defenders and let the clock run down. Then, suddenly, Zack flew toward the goal, dribbling hard and fast to escape the Sharks defense. Glancing to his right, Zack spied Mario slicing toward the goal. But the Sharks goalie saw Mario, too.

Zack fired the ball to the left, past the

Sharks defense. Cougars midfielder Nate Tanzi raced in and blasted the ball into the net.

"Goooaaaal!" Tyler shouted again, with a big, happy grin. *Man, Zack has moves!* he thought.

"All right, Nate!" Coach Murray shouted, jumping in the air. "Nice ball, Zack."

After the game, as Tyler, Mario, and Zack gathered up their things, Coach Murray walked over and said, "Good game, guys. You were awesome today. We'll definitely be ready for the regular season."

"When's our first game, again, Coach?" Tyler asked.

"Right here, next Saturday—a week from today—at two o'clock. I'll give out schedules at Wednesday's practice. Team rosters will be posted on the league's website tomorrow. See you Wednesday." She headed off to the parking lot with a bag of soccer balls slung over her shoulder.

Tyler and his friends stayed at the edge of the field, reliving the game.

"That first goal was sweet," Tyler said.

Zack shrugged. "I could have scored *five* goals against those guys. The Sharks aren't very good."

Tyler smiled to himself. *Just like Zack. Always thinking he's the best,* he thought.

"The Sharks weren't so bad," Mario said.

"What do you mean?" Zack said. "I hardly broke a sweat playing them."

"So how come your shirt is so wet?" Tyler asked, pulling at Zack's damp soccer shirt. "And smelly, too. Oooo-weeee!"

Mario laughed, but Zack flicked Tyler's hand off his shirt. "Cut it out," he said.

Just then Zack's dad walked up. "Good game, guys. Hey, Zack, Mr. Wexler wants to talk to you."

"Where is he?" Zack asked, looking around.

"Back on the field, near the far goal."

"Okay." Zack headed back toward the field with his father. "I'll see you tomorrow," he called back to Tyler and Mario.

"See ya." Tyler waved.

The two boys trudged slowly toward the parking lot. "Who's Mr. Wexler?" Tyler asked Mario.

"He's the coach of the Putty Hill Panthers," Mario said. "You know, that travel team with all the hotshot players?"

"Oh yeah." Tyler nodded. He knew they played on the high school field and wore uniforms that looked like the ones the pros wear. "I wonder what he wants with Zack."

"What do you *think* he wants?" Mario said. "He's been bugging Zack to play for the Panthers for years."

Tyler looked off toward the field and spotted Zack and his dad talking to Mr. Wexler. "Zack wouldn't leave the Cougars for the Panthers," he said. "We've got the perfect team."

Chapter 2

Tyler saw the football spiraling through the Sunday afternoon sunshine. He reached up with both hands, pulled it from the sky, and raced down the field. "Touchdown!" he shouted as he crossed into the end zone, holding the football high above his head.

"You pushed off," Devante Watson protested. "Pass interference."

"I didn't push off," Tyler insisted. "Don't be a wimp."

Devante looked to the other two players for support. Ben Rosen and Ramon Campos just rolled their eyes. "Come on, let's keep playing," said Ben.

Devante got madder. "You guys all play

on the Cougars. That's why you're siding with Tyler. I'm telling you, it was definitely pass interference."

Just then Mario arrived at the field.

"Did you see that last play?" Devante asked him.

"Yeah, I saw it," Mario said.

"He pushed off," Devante said, pointing at Tyler. He thrust his hands up and away from his chest to demonstrate. "That's offensive-pass interference!"

"Wait a second," Tyler broke in. "Mario saw the play. Let him make the call."

Mario paused, pretending to think. He looked at Tyler and then at Devante. Then he shouted, "Touchdown!"

Devante turned away in disgust. "No way, man," he said. "You and Tyler always stick together. That was pass interference."

"Come on, Devante," Tyler said. "It's not even a real game. We're just fooling around until Zack shows up."

"Hey, guess what I've got," Mario said, changing the subject. He waved some papers in front of the boys.

"What?"

"The soccer league rosters."

"Who cares?" Devante said, frowning. "I don't even play soccer. We're supposed to be playing football, remember?"

The boys ignored him and crowded around Mario as he unfolded the rosters.

"We're stacked," Tyler said, reading over Mario's shoulder. "We have Zack, Justin, Nate, Mario, Ben, Ramon, and me..."

COUGARS	MUD DOGS
Coach: Ms. Suzanne Murray	**Coach:** Mr. Michael Wilden
Players:	**Players:**
Zachary Bell	Jackson Bland
Ramon Campos	Charles Coe
Christopher Chen	Casey DeCamp
Mario Cruz	George Drumheller
Tyler Davis	Sean Gates
Joshua Matta	Collin Gillis
Patrick McCracken	Richard Harris
Eric Palmer	Daniel Landwehr
Ben Rosen	Michael Li
Justin Sheridan	Lee Mathews
John Shortall	Martin Reyes
Nathan Tanzi	Stephen Thomas
Ricardo Watts	Bobby Wilden

"The Mud Dogs look good, too," Mario pointed out. "They've got Casey DeCamp, George Drumheller, Collin Gillis, Martin Reyes, and Bobby Wilden."

"No way they can beat us," Tyler said, dismissing the thought with a wave. "They don't have anyone who can cover Zack. He's the best player in the league. And we've got Nate and Justin."

"How about the Mustangs?" Ben asked. "They look good."

"Well, okay," Tyler said. "Maybe one or two teams have a chance of beating us. But only a couple."

"Don't be too sure," Mario warned.

"Yeah," Devante put in. "You might lose a game because the ref makes a lousy call. Like pass interference."

"Will you forget the pass interference?" Mario said.

Tyler tapped the roster sheet. "I bet we'll win the league," he said. "And then we'll get to play in the County Cup with all the other town champs."

"Yeah, but the County Cup has travel teams in it, too," Ben said.

"And one of them usually wins the County Cup," Mario said. "Those travel teams are like all-stars. They're really good."

Tyler shrugged off Mario's opinion. "We can play with them. Especially if we've got Zack."

"Speaking of playing," Devante said as he held up the football. "Hel-looooo? How about getting back to football?"

"We've only got five players," Tyler said. "You can't have fair teams with five."

"What if one of us plays permanent quarterback?" Devante pleaded.

"Permanent quarterback stinks," Tyler said.

"Where's Zack?" Mario asked, looking around.

"I don't know," Tyler said. "I told him we were playing at two o'clock. What time is it now?"

"It doesn't matter. Why don't *you* start at permanent quarterback?" Devante asked. "That way you can't push off and commit pass interference."

"Hey, there's Zack," Tyler said.

Everyone turned and saw Zack riding his bike toward them. Zack pulled to a stop, hopped off his bike, and let it fall to the ground. Tyler raced over to Zack and handed him the roster. "Mario got all the team rosters," he said. "Man, we are so sweet."

"Yeah, we're loaded," Mario said.

Zack stared blankly at the Cougars roster. Finally he looked up and said, "I'm not playing."

"What? You mean football?" Tyler asked.

"No." Zack handed the roster back to Tyler. "I mean I'm not playing for the Cougars this year."

Chapter 3

"What do you mean, you're not playing?" Tyler blurted out. "Are you moving?" Ben asked.

"What's wrong?" asked Mario. "Are you sick or something?"

"Are you flunking math?" Tyler asked.

"No...no...no...," Zack said. "I'm playing for the Putty Hill Panthers."

Tyler's mouth dropped open in surprise. "*What?* Since when?"

"Since yesterday. Coach Wexler asked me and Justin and Nate to join the team."

"Justin and Nate, too?" Tyler gasped. Mario and Ben groaned.

Zack nodded.

"And you guys said *yes*?" Tyler couldn't believe what he was hearing.

"Yeah."

"Can you maybe play for both teams?" Mario asked desperately.

"You can't do that. It's against the rules," Zack said. "And anyway, the Panthers have more practices and they have games or a tournament every weekend. There's no way I could play for both."

Tyler looked back at the Cougars roster and imagined the list without the names Zack Bell, Justin Sheridan, and Nate Tanzi.

Without them, the Cougars roster looked a lot less sweet. There was no way they'd get to the County Cup now.

"It's gonna be great. Coach Wexler really wants me for the team, but I've always said no before," Zack said quickly, his words tumbling over one another. "The Panthers have lost some players this season, and they need me as a midfielder. Justin will play striker."

Tyler could barely stand hearing about the Panthers. It wasn't fair, Zack changing teams right before the Cougars season. "What about us?" Tyler demanded. "We were going to have a great team."

"You guys will still be really good," Zack insisted. "You've got Mario and you..." He looked down at the roster. "Hey, you might even get to play my position: attacking midfielder."

"We were gonna play together," Tyler said, "all the way through high school."

"We'll still play together in high school," Zack said.

Tyler started breathing slow and hard. He could feel the anger rising higher and higher inside him.

"Come on, Ty," Zack said, beginning to sound impatient. "The Panthers have better coaches—"

"Coach Murray is a really good coach," Mario insisted. "She played on a college soccer team."

"Yeah, but the players in the travel league are better, too. I mean, our game on Saturday was an easy win," Zack said.

"There are some decent teams in our league," Tyler said. "The Mud Dogs are pretty good. And the Mustangs—"

Zack rolled his eyes and shook his head.

"Come on, none of those guys are any good," he said. "There's no way they could play for the Panthers."

"The Panthers aren't so great," Tyler snapped.

"You're just jealous that Mr. Wexler didn't ask *you* to be on the team," Zack shot back.

"What's that supposed to mean?" Tyler demanded.

But before Zack could answer, Mario said, "Hey, Ty, Zack's right. I mean, the Panthers are pretty good. Anyone would want to play for them."

"What?" said Tyler. "Since when are you on *his* side?"

"He isn't on my *side!* It's just the truth!" Zack shouted. "The Panthers are a great team. And sorry, but Mr. Wexler didn't pick either of you guys. He picked me and Justin and Nate."

"Hey, come on, Zack," Mario said. "You don't have to rub it in."

"Okay, but it's the truth." Then Zack lowered his voice and spoke more slowly.

"Look, I really want to play travel soccer, okay? They play more games and go to tournaments and stuff. The Panthers won the County Cup a couple years ago."

"You may not get a chance to play that much," Mario pointed out. "The Panthers probably have somebody good at attacking midfielder."

"Then he'd better move over," Zack said, with a confident smile.

"I can't believe this!" Tyler said. "We've played together since second grade. And you're breaking up the team!"

"You still have a team," Zack said. The two of them stood just a few paces apart, staring at each other. "I'm just on another team," Zack said finally. "That's all."

"Okay, okay," Mario said, stepping between the two boys. "It's done. There's nothing you can do about it, Ty. Zack is playing for the Panthers and that's that."

"Yeah," Devante said. "So let's play some touch football."

"Fine," Mario said. "How about me, Devante, and Ben against you guys?"

Tyler felt his muscles tighten. He didn't want to be on Zack's team. Not now. Not after Zack had said he was leaving the Cougars. It would be like playing with a traitor.

"I can't play," Zack said as he got back on his bike. "I've got practice at three o'clock."

"It's only a little after two," Devante said. "We can get in a quick game."

Zack shook his head. "Nope. Coach Wexler wants us to get there early so we can stretch. I can't be late my first day."

"Man, we can't play with five," Devante complained. "It's not as much fun with five."

Still mad, Tyler kept quiet. He didn't want to play football with Zack anyway.

"I gotta go," Zack said. He pedaled away across the open field.

Tyler watched him ride off as the other boys argued about playing football with just five players. He felt like Zack was riding away with the whole Cougars soccer season.

Chapter 4

Tweeeeeeet! Coach Murray's whistle cut through the warm autumn air. "All right, everybody," she called. "Bring it in."

The Cougars stopped stretching, jogged to the goalpost, and gathered in front of their coach. Tyler looked around at the players. The team seemed so much smaller without Zack, Justin, and Nate. It hardly seemed like a team at all.

Tyler turned back to Coach Murray. As usual, her dark ponytail poked out through the back of her red visor. She didn't look mad or even frustrated. It was as if nothing had happened to their team. "Okay, guys," she said in her matter-of-fact way. "I'm sure you've heard by now that Zack, Justin, and Nate have decided to play for the Putty Hill Panthers..."

Tyler scanned his teammates. The Cougars were all nodding. Everyone had already heard the news.

"So," Coach continued, "we're going to get three new players—"

"Do we know who they are, Coach?" Ramon, the Cougars goalie, asked.

"Not yet," she answered as she took a swig from her water bottle. "But the league promised me new players by Saturday's game. There are still some kids in town who haven't been placed on a team."

"Leftovers," Tyler whispered to Mario.

"Yeah," Mario agreed.

"There's no way they're gonna be as good as Zack," Tyler whispered back, still looking at Coach Murray.

"So that means we're going to have to make some changes," Coach went on. She looked down at her clipboard. "Okay. Let's try Tyler at Zack's old position..."

Tyler's head popped back. He had always

dreamed of playing attacking midfielder. Being attacking midfielder was like being a point guard in basketball or a quarterback in football. The attacking midfielder was always in the middle of the action. He practically ran the team. But Tyler had never had the chance to play that position with Zack around.

Mario elbowed him in the ribs. "You're the new Zack Bell. All right!"

Coach wasn't finished. "Mario, why don't you move to striker, Justin's old spot?" she said, looking down at her clipboard. "And Josh, you're in Nate's position, center midfielder."

Mario and Josh Matta traded high fives with some of the other Cougars.

"Who are we playing Saturday?" Chris Chen, the Cougars rock-solid sweeper, asked.

"The Tazmaniacs," Coach answered. "We beat them 2–0 last year, but it's a whole new season. Everybody's starting over." She set down her clipboard and waved the players onto the field. "Okay, back to work! Let's start with our passing drill," she called out.

"I want three lines: left, middle, and right. Josh, Tyler, and Mario, you're in the middle line. Let's go."

Tyler knew the Cougars passing drill by heart. They started almost every practice with it. Three players—one from each line—moved quickly down the field. The guy on the left passed the ball to the guy in the middle, who passed the ball to the guy on the right. Then they reversed the play—right to middle, middle to left—and started all over again, always advancing toward the goal. Touch, pass, charge ahead. Touch, pass, charge ahead.

Done right, the ball and the players never stopped moving—all the way down the field and back. But today the drill was different. Tyler could sense it as he watched the first group move down the field with Josh in the middle, passing to the left and right wings.

Josh didn't seem quick or sure of himself in the middle.

"It's going to feel kind of funny to be in the middle on the passing drill," Mario said to Tyler as their three teammates reached the end of the field and turned back.

"Yeah," Tyler agreed as he watched the ball pass between the middle and outside lanes. "Coach always put Zack and Justin in the middle and us on the wings."

"I guess we'd better get used to the middle," Mario said.

Suddenly the ball was at Tyler's feet and it was his group's turn to go. Coach Murray ran along the side of the field, shouting instructions to Tyler, Ben, and Chris. "Come on, move up. Stay ahead of the ball, Ty. Both feet, Ben, both feet. Head up, Chris. Come on!" At the end of the field, Tyler spun around and headed back. He slid the ball to Chris on his right and raced ahead. Chris passed it back to Tyler in the middle lane. Touch, pass, charge ahead.

Tyler stopped the ball with his left foot. With a quick half step, he nudged the ball forward, checked his left, and angled a pass to Ben.

"Keep moving, Tyler!" Coach shouted. "Keep moving!"

Ben controlled the ball and knocked it back into the middle lane.

Tyler sprinted toward the ball just as it was about to whiz by him. He got his right foot on the ball, but it was spinning too fast, and his foot rolled right over it. Then his left foot tangled with the ball and there was nowhere to go but down. He tried to turn his shoulder to roll with the fall, but everything was moving too fast.

Thwump! Tyler's chest and chin hit the ground. He scrambled to his feet, out of breath and embarrassed.

Coach Murray was still shouting along the sidelines. "Get up! Don't wait for a whistle. Keep going."

Tyler managed to pass the ball to Mario, who led the next group down the field. Tyler took his place behind Josh and immediately bent over to rest his hands on his thighs and catch his breath.

"Come on, Mario. Keep it moving," Coach Murray called out. She turned to look at Tyler. "Are you okay?" she asked.

Tyler waved his hand without looking up.

"Nice face-plant, Ty," Josh teased.

Tyler stood up and stretched, as if checking to see if all his parts were still working. "Yeah, that was real smooth," he said, smiling slightly. "I gotta score that a 9.8."

"No way, Ty, that was a perfect 10," Josh said, laughing. "Better wipe your chin, you cut yourself."

Tyler wiped his chin and looked at the streak of red on the back of his hand. *Guess I'm definitely not as good as Zack,* he thought. *Zack never fell on his face.*

"This being-in-the-middle stuff is a lot trickier than being on the side," Josh said. "Man, Zack made it look so easy."

"No kidding," Tyler muttered under his breath.

The practice went on and on. More passing drills. Centering passes. Corner kicks. Clearing passes. Back passes. Free kicks. Penalty kicks. And finally, a quick scrimmage. Coach Murray had the Cougars working hard so they would be ready for their opening game.

After practice, Tyler lay back on the warm

grass, staring up at the sky. "When's your Mom picking us up?" he asked Mario.

Mario pulled his phone from the front pocket of his backpack. "In about fifteen minutes. She's got to pick up my little brother at baseball practice first."

"I wish I played baseball," Tyler sighed.

"I thought you didn't like baseball," Mario said, putting his phone back.

"I don't. But there's no way anyone can get this tired playing baseball." Tyler lifted his head and rested back on his elbows.

"So how'd you like playing in the middle?" Mario asked.

"It was kind of cool." Tyler grinned. "After I stopped falling on my face."

"Yeah," Mario said. "I think I'm going to like being the striker."

Tyler took a deep breath and blew it out in a rush. "Well, I sure didn't make anybody forget Zack Bell today."

"You'll be all right," Mario said. "You just have to get used to playing in the middle and seeing the whole field."

Tyler flopped back down on the grass.

"The rest of the team didn't look so hot either."

"We'll be okay. It was just our first practice without Zack and the other guys."

"We'd better get it together before we play the Tazmaniacs on Saturday," Tyler said, still looking at the sky. "At least they're not very good."

"What do you mean? They're okay."

Tyler closed his eyes. "Then we're in big trouble," he said.

Chapter 5

Tyler was practically out of the car before it stopped. "See ya," he said quickly to his parents and raced down the small hill to the soccer field.

Everything was ready for the first game of the season. Fresh lines of white paint streaked the bright green grass. The coaches had stretched the orange netting onto the silver metal goals. The yellow corner flags flapped in the breeze. Parents and other fans clustered along the sidelines.

All the Cougars were dressed in uniform—blue-and-white T-shirts, dark blue shorts, and white socks. Tyler ran to join his teammates on the field, where they were passing balls in small circles to warm up for the game. Across the field, wearing orange T-shirts, white shorts, and orange socks, the Tazmaniacs were doing the same.

"Come on, Cougars," Coach Murray called a few minutes later through cupped hands. "Bring it in." The team gathered in front of her. "Okay," she said, pointing her clipboard toward three boys who stood nervously beside her. "These are the new players I was telling you about." She placed her hands on each boy's shoulders as she introduced him. "This is Mikey Thomson. David Marshall. And Gavin Sheridan. Let's give them a Cougars welcome!"

"Leftovers," Mario muttered to Tyler as the two of them clapped in unison with their teammates.

"They'd better not be," Tyler said. As he continued to clap, he looked more closely at the new players. Two were medium height and skinny. Gavin was slightly shorter. He looked strong, but a little younger than the others. "Hey, isn't that Gavin kid Justin's little brother?" Tyler whispered to Mario.

"I think so."

"He's only a sixth grader," Tyler said, feeling a little annoyed.

"Yeah, but maybe he's good," Mario said as the clapping died down. "His brother's a player. That's why the Panthers wanted him."

"I hope Gavin's a player then, too."

"Okay, let's get started." Coach Murray nodded toward the new players. "I'll try to work in you three as the game goes on." Then the referee blew his whistle and Coach started talking fast to the whole team. "Remember, Mario, you're in Justin's old spot at striker. Tyler, you're in Zack's, attacking midfielder." She glanced down at her clipboard and added, "Josh, you're in Nate's old spot, as center midfielder."

The referee blew his whistle again, more loudly this time.

"All right, everybody, hands together." Coach Murray put her hand into the circle. The Cougars piled their hands on top. The three new players were the last to join in. "First game of the season, so let's play hard the whole game," Coach said. "On the count of three: one...two...three..."

"Hustle!" all the Cougars yelled—except the three new players. Then the starting players ran out to their positions on the field.

The Cougars tried to hustle, but nothing seemed to click. Their passes were too long or too wide. They couldn't keep up any kind of attack. But neither could the Tazmaniacs. The game lurched back and forth like a tug-of-war contest that neither side could win.

Tyler struggled at midfield. Whenever he passed the ball ahead to Mario or one of the wings, nothing happened. No goals. No shots. No threats to score.

Finally Tyler tried to take control. He intercepted a pass and darted around a surprised Tazmaniac. Instead of passing the ball up to the forwards, Tyler pressed on, dribbling around defenders and moving closer to the goal.

About 20 yards out, Tyler darted to his left and then spun back to his right, hoping to fire off a quick shot. As he twirled around, a Tazmaniac defender reached out with his foot. He missed the ball but clipped Tyler's ankle.

Tyler tumbled onto the ball, skidding hands-first along the grass. The ball squirted forward and a Tazmaniac defender lofted a long kick away from the goal.

Tyler scrambled to his knees and glared at the referee. "How about a foul?" he called, smacking the ground with both hands.

"Play on," the referee said and ran down the field, following the ball and the action.

"Get up, get up!" Coach Murray called.

Tyler threw down two fistfuls of dirt, but bounced up and sprinted back to help on defense.

The first half ended in a scoreless tie.

Coach Murray tried to rally the Cougars as they sat on the sidelines, gulping water and breathing hard. "Remember, don't bunch up. Spread across the field and keep moving the ball around. Short, crisp passes. Tyler, keep passing the ball to the forwards.

Don't try to dribble through the entire defense."

Tyler looked down and shook his head. *Playing the middle is tough,* he thought. *Zack really messed things up when he left the team!*

The second half was no better than the first. Gavin, one of the new Cougars, showed he had some of his brother's speed and cool moves along the wing. But the rest of the Cougars weren't used to playing with him, and their passes failed to connect. The game was a big muddle in the middle of the field. Tyler wished it were over. He wanted to take the scoreless tie and run home.

"Come on, Cougars!" Coach Murray shouted. "Five minutes left. Hang in there."

A Tazmaniacs defender boomed a long kick toward the Cougars goal. Cougars defender Ben Rosen and a Tazmaniac forward both jumped up to head the ball. It skidded off the back of Ben's head and bounced to the corner.

Sensing the play, a Tazmaniac midfielder ran to the corner, then spun and kicked the ball to a teammate hovering near the goal. Ramon, the Cougars goalie, moved out to grab the pass. But he collided with the Cougars sweeper, Chris Chen. The ball bounced wildly across the mouth of the goal as Tyler and a dozen other players raced in. The Tazmaniacs left wing won the race and sent the ball spinning into the left corner of the Cougars net.

The Cougars were behind, 1–0!

The Cougars tried to fight back. Tyler stole a pass and dribbled past two defenders. He rocketed a shot at the upper right corner of the goal, but the ball sailed wide. Tyler bent over and slapped the side of his legs. He sensed that the Cougars' last, best chance was gone. The Cougars hadn't had many shots on the Tazmaniacs goal. Time was running out and Tyler doubted they would get any more. A minute later, the referee blew the whistle and waved his arms above his head.

The game was over. The Cougars had lost their first game of the season, 1–0.

After shaking hands with all the happy

Tazmaniacs, the Cougars players, coaches, and parents walked in small groups to the parking lot. Tyler and Mario walked side by side with their heads down.

"Looks like you guys could have used me today," a familiar voice said. The boys looked up and saw Zack standing at the corner of the field, smiling.

"Hey, Zack." Mario waved. "Yeah, we could've used you, all right."

Tyler glared at Mario. He didn't want Zack thinking the Cougars were falling apart. "Give us a break, Zack. We're just getting used to our new positions," he said, still walking.

"Yeah, I could tell," Zack said, catching up. "You know what you need to do at midfield? You've got to let the game come to you."

Tyler quickened his pace as Zack kept talking. "Don't try to force things," he went on. "Keep the ball moving, but when you see an opening, go for it. Like I did in the second half of that first preseason game. Remember?"

Tyler remembered. He also remembered how Zack always liked to tell people what to do. It hadn't been so bad when Zack was on the Cougars and scoring goals for them. But right now Tyler felt like telling his old friend to get lost.

"And try to get the ball to Justin's little brother," Zack went on. "What's his name… Gavin? He looks really fast."

Tyler didn't answer. He kept walking a few steps ahead of Zack and Mario.

"Hey, you guys should come to the Panthers' first game tonight," Zack said.

"Where are you playing?" Mario asked.

"At the high school, eight o'clock," Zack said. "Under the lights."

"Sounds cool," Mario said, looking at Tyler.

"I don't know," Tyler mumbled. "See ya." He waved at his parents in the parking lot and jogged up the hill.

Chapter 6

Tyler's father stopped the car near the high school field to let Tyler and Mario out. "How long will the game last?" he asked.

"Probably about an hour and a half," Tyler answered.

"Okay, I've got to go by Software City. I'll meet you back here in an hour and a half. Got it?"

The boys nodded, then headed down the sidewalk and into a short, dark tunnel.

"Why did I let you talk me into coming to this?" Tyler said, sending Mario a sideways glance.

"Come on, Ty, it'll be fun," Mario said as they entered the bright high school stadium and heard the pounding rock music.

Tyler angled his left hand against the glare of the lights and took in the scene. Two teams in shiny uniforms were warming up, one at either end of the field. Men rolled out the goals and placed them carefully on the two end lines. Fans filled the stands on both sides of the field, eager for the game to begin.

He looked up at the electronic scoreboard. "The game's going to start in about three minutes," he said.

Mario looked around at the lights and the scoreboard and the teams as they walked toward the grandstand. "Pretty cool," he said. "Like a college game or something."

Tyler looked across the field and thought back to the Cougars game against the Tazmaniacs, with the taped-on nets and people standing around the field. "Yeah," he said. "It's like it's more official…more big-league than our games."

"I guess Zack made the right move by switching teams," Mario said.

"No way," Tyler replied, frowning. "He should have stuck with his real team."

The boys ran up the stadium steps, taking them two at a time.

"Hey, Ty. Hey, Mario." Zack's mom and dad were sitting in the middle of a group of other parents.

"Hi, Mr. Bell, Mrs. Bell." Tyler waved back.

"How'd the Cougars do this afternoon?" Mr. Bell asked.

Tyler tried to act as if he didn't care. "We lost 1–0."

"Too bad, guys," Mr. Bell said. "Hang in there. Say hi to your mom and dad, Ty."

Tyler and Mario nodded. Then they scooted into the first empty row above the other Putty Hill Panthers fans.

An older man in a rumpled tweed sport coat and battered cap walked slowly up the stadium steps. A lot of the fans seemed to know him.

"Hello, Mr. Robertson."

"Welcome back, Nigel," another mom called out.

"Good to see you again, Mr. Robertson."

Mr. Robertson smiled and lifted a hand in a small greeting. He reached the row where Tyler and Mario were sitting and pointed at the end of the bench. "Is anyone sitting here, lads?" he asked in a clear English accent.

"No," Tyler and Mario answered together as the man sat down. The boys stretched out, leaning against the bench in back of them, and settled in to watch the Panthers play the Glenwood Tigers.

The game started quickly. Both teams passed the ball briskly and attacked the goal whenever they had a chance.

"Where is Zack playing?" Tyler asked.

"Looks like right wing," Mario said.

"Told you he wouldn't play midfield." Tyler smiled to himself.

Below on the field, Zack spun around a Tigers defender and dribbled downfield. He darted to his right and curved a long pass toward the left wing. The Panthers forward easily controlled the pass and left-footed the ball toward the net. The crowd groaned as the ball skidded past the far post.

"What a shot!" Tyler yelled, springing to his feet. But he quickly sat back down when he remembered how mad he was at Zack.

"Wow. Zack led him perfectly with the pass," Mario said.

Mr. Robertson looked over at the boys. "The keeper played that just right," he said, pointing toward the goal. "Cut down the angle so he had to shoot it wide. That was brilliant."

The Panthers kept the pressure on, moving the ball around the edge of the penalty box as they searched for an opening. Finally, toward the end of the first half, they scored on a header that sent the ball into the upper reaches of the net.

Mario jumped up when the Panthers scored and turned to trade high fives with Tyler. But Tyler was still sitting on the bench, his hands thrust deep in his pockets. It seemed strange to look out at the Panthers and see Zack celebrating with another team.

At the half, Tyler and Mario talked about the game.

"It's a pretty good match," Mario said.

"Yeah, the ball is really moving," Tyler agreed. "But the Panthers aren't all that much better than us."

"I don't know," Mario said. "Some of those guys look pretty good."

"Zack is just as good as any of them, and he used to be a Cougar like us," Tyler pointed out.

"Yeah, that's true. He was our best player, though." Mario stood up. "I'm going to buy a soda. Want one?"

Tyler stayed on the bench. "No thanks," he said, crossing his arms. "I'll stay here." He didn't feel like running into Zack down near the field.

The second half started with the Tigers pressing the attack against the Panthers. Early in the half a Tigers header sailed just over the crossbar. "The Panthers had better watch their step," Mr. Robertson told the boys. "The Tigers are picking up the pace."

The old man started shouting instructions as if he were coaching the game. "Come on, center pass. Center pass...stay back...oh, head up. He's open on the right wing." Mr. Robertson jumped up, threw his hands into the air, and sat down again, shaking his head.

"Do you have a kid on one of the teams?" Tyler asked.

"No," the man said. "I just love football."

Tyler and Mario looked at each other, then at Mr. Roberston. "But this is soccer," Mario said.

"Sorry. That's what I meant." The man smiled. "We call it football in England." He nodded toward the field. "Do you know anybody out there?" he asked.

"Number nine on the wing for the Panthers," Tyler said as Zack raced up the sideline with the ball at his feet.

"He's a good player, a good ball handler." Mr. Robertson nodded. "They should play him in the middle." He eyed Tyler and Mario. "Why aren't you lads in this game?"

"We play for another team," Mario said.

"I see. Do you think you could you beat these teams?" the old man asked.

Tyler studied the field as Zack trapped a ball with his chest, slid a quick pass to another Panther, and raced up the field. He wanted to say yes, but he wasn't sure. "I don't know," he answered.

“Pfffft,” Mr. Robertson said with a wave of his hand. “Any team can beat another. That’s the great thing about football.”

“What do you mean?” Tyler asked.

The old man pointed at the scoreboard. “What’s the score?” he demanded.

“One to nothing,” said Tyler. The score was right there in bright orange numbers. Maybe the man couldn’t see very well.

“And how many football matches are decided by one goal?” Mr. Robertson said.

“Lots,” Tyler and Mario answered together.

The man held up one finger. “So that means most games are decided by one play. A head ball, a brilliant goal, or a great save.” He pointed toward the boys. “Just one play,” he repeated, and looked back at the field.

Mario arched his eyebrows as if to say to Tyler: *Is he for real?* Mr. Robertson didn’t seem to notice and kept talking. “I remember when I was about your age, our English lads had the best football—I mean soccer—team in the world.” He gazed at the field, but seemed to be remembering long ago. "Everyone thought they were going to win the World Cup. They played the Americans in the first round."

"Were the Americans any good?" Tyler asked.

"No!" Mr. Robertson thundered, startling the boys.

Whoa, this guy takes soccer pretty seriously, Tyler thought.

"There was no way the Americans should have won that match," the old man said. "They were a bunch of college mates and semipros playing the best professional footballers in England—maybe the world."

"You mean America won?" Mario asked.

Mr. Robertson nodded. "One to nothing."

"How'd they beat the English guys?" Tyler asked.

"They played more like a team. Joe Gaetjens was brilliant."

"Who?" Tyler blurted.

"Joe Gaetjens," Mr. Robertson repeated. "G-A-E-T-J-E-N-S. I'll never forget that name. Scored a goal on a header in the first half. Came flying out of nowhere. The English team tried to come back, but the American keeper, a fellow named Frank Borghi, made some beautiful saves." The old man took a deep breath.

"In any case, the people back home in England couldn't believe it. Our lads, the best in the world, beaten by a bunch of Yanks—that's what we Brits called the Americans. Why, hardly any Americans even played football—er, soccer—back then." He turned to the boys and held up one finger again. "But the Americans made the one play they needed to win the game."

Tyler thought about what the old man had said. "Yeah, but there are a whole lot of plays in a soccer game," he said finally.

"Ah, yes," Mr. Robertson said, his eyes glued on the action below where the Tigers were threatening to score. "But in most games, only one play makes the difference."

"How do you know which play is going to make the difference?" Tyler asked.

"You don't," Mr. Robertson said, smiling. "So you have to hustle on every ball as if it's the play that will change the game. That's exactly what those Americans did. They hustled every minute."

On the field the Tigers sent a crossing pass sailing toward the goal. A Tigers player leaped between two Panthers defenders, craned his neck, and headed the ball toward the goal. The Panthers goalie leaped to the side, stretched as far as he could, and fisted the ball over the top of the net. The Panthers were still ahead, 1–0.

Mr. Robertson leaned back and smiled. "What did I tell you? Sometimes it takes just one play."

Tyler stared out at the floodlit field, watching as the Panthers clung to their one-goal lead and claimed their victory. He kept thinking about what the old man had said. Could one play change the Cougars' season—even without Zack?

Chapter 7

Yeah, in about half an hour," Tyler said into his phone as he walked around the living room. "Green Street Park."

Across the room, Mario spoke into another phone. "Thirty minutes. The whole team's gonna be there. Okay? See you there." He reached out his hand to Tyler. "Give me the list, Ty," he demanded. "Have you called Josh?"

Tyler handed him the list of names and phone numbers and shook his head. "Not yet. Why don't you call Josh and Ben and that new kid, Gavin?"

For the next few minutes their voices blended as they finished making calls to the team.

"Yeah. Green Street in around twenty-five minutes."

"We've got a ball. Just bring your cleats."

"Can't you skip piano practice? Tell your mom you'll practice double tomorrow."

"Come on, you're not gonna get any better playing video games."

"No, of course you don't have to wear your uniform. It's just a pickup game."

An hour later, Tyler stood surrounded by ten boys at Green Street Park. "I've got Ramon, Ben, Gavin, and Josh," Tyler said, pointing at his teammates. "Mario, you've got the rest." He walked to the end of the field and placed sweatshirts in two piles about five feet apart. "This is our goal," he called. "Mario, you make one down at your end."

"Any goalies?" Ramon asked.

"No goalies," Tyler said. "Everybody can play in the field. Ramon, you play back with Ben. I'll play mid. Josh and Gavin will be forwards."

Soon the ball was flashing back and forth between the teams, and shouts filled the field.

"Come on, move the ball around."

"Hustle, don't let him get it."

"Get back, get back."

"Back to the middle," Tyler called. Ben bounced him a pass. Tyler trapped the ball and looked up the field. He spun around one defender and angled a pass to his left where Gavin had sprinted past a surprised Chris Chen. Gavin raced toward the goal. A defender threatened him, but he managed a swift pass to Tyler, who left-footed a low shot between the sweatshirt goalposts.

"Goooaaal!" Tyler shouted as he dropped to his knees for a dramatic skid into the grass.

"Come on, Ty," Mario snapped. "What do you think this is, the World Cup? It's just one goal."

Tyler laughed as he got to his feet. "I know," he said. "But did you see that pass from Freddy here?"

"I'm Gavin," Gavin corrected, looking confused.

Tyler's smile widened. "Nah. The way you run, you're more like Freddy Adu," he said, jogging alongside Gavin as the team ran back down the field.

"You mean the pro soccer star?" Gavin asked.

"Yep," Tyler said. "Fast Freddy Adu. That's you."

"Hey, can I play?" Zack stood at the edge of the field in silk soccer shorts, cleats, and a yellow practice jersey.

Tyler stopped in the middle of the field. He didn't want Zack barging in on their game. The whole point was for the Cougars to get better, not Zack. "We've already got teams," he said.

"Mario's team has six players," Zack pointed out. "It'll be six-on-six if I play for your team. Come on, are you afraid I'll make the teams uneven?"

Tyler felt his face get hot. *That's just like Zack,* he thought. *Always thinking he's the best.*

"Forget it," Tyler said. "We're practicing. This is *our* team."

"Come on," Zack said. "I just want to play for a little while. I've got practice with the Panthers in twenty minutes."

"So can we practice with the Panthers later, then?" Tyler snapped.

"Okay, forget it," Zack said, as he started go. Then he turned around and asked, "Do you think you guys could keep up with the Panthers?"

"Maybe," Tyler said, not sure if it was really true. "If we got the chance."

"Who knows? Maybe you *will* get the chance," Zack said. Then he left.

"What did he mean by that?" Tyler said, frowning.

Mario shrugged. "Who cares? Let's just play."

The Cougars continued their pickup scrimmage. They played at top speed for almost two hours.

Passing.

Shooting.

Shouting.

Sweating.

Finally some parents began collecting their kids from the park. The other players picked up the sweatshirts from the dirt and their water bottles from the sidelines and scattered slowly into the deepening twilight.

"See you later, Freddy," Tyler called. "Good game."

Gavin smiled and waved. "It was fun."

"He can really play for a sixth grader," Mario said as he and Tyler walked slowly home.

"Yeah," Tyler agreed. "He'll give us some real speed. The other two new guys, Mikey and David, are pretty good, too."

"Not as good as Zack and Justin," Mario said.

Tyler wiped the sweat from his forehead with his sweatshirt. "Not yet. But they're gonna be okay. Wait and see."

"At least we didn't get a bunch of losers," Mario said. "Who do we play Saturday?"

"The Hornets."

"I don't remember them much."

"We beat 'em 2–1 last year. But it was a tough game."

"We can keep practicing on our own like we did this afternoon, I guess," Mario said. "Everybody said they wanted to."

"Yeah," Tyler agreed. "I need the extra

practice to get used to playing midfield."

"You looked pretty okay today. You were passing the ball like a regular Zack Bell."

"Can you believe Zack tried to barge in on our practice?" Tyler said. He spat out a mouthful of water on the dirt.

"He wasn't trying to barge in," Mario protested. "He just wanted to play."

"Well, he's got his own team. He should go play with them."

Mario shook his head. "C'mon Tyler. Give Zack a break. He's our friend," he said. "So he went to the Panthers. Can you blame him? You said yourself that the Panthers were more big-league."

"Yeah, but now that he's on a travel team, he's acting like he's super cool," Tyler said.

"He's not so bad," Mario said. "Anyway, maybe you'd act like that, too, if the Panthers had asked you to play for them."

"No way," Tyler blurted out. But secretly he thought Mario might be right. Maybe he should let up on Zack and concentrate on the Cougars. Otherwise they were never going to win.

The two boys walked in silence for a long block. The first fallen leaves crunched hard and dry beneath their feet. "We'd better win on Saturday," Tyler said finally. "It would be really hard to make the County Cup after two straight losses. They only take teams that win their leagues."

"And some travel teams," Mario said. "Like the Panthers."

Tyler didn't answer.

"I know what you're thinking," Mario said. "If we make it into the County Cup, we might get to play Zack's team. You think we can beat them?"

"Hey," Tyler said, shrugging. "Like that old guy Mr. Robertson said, 'Anything can happen.'"

Chapter 8

Tyler heard the wind the moment he woke up on Saturday morning. The leaves whipped around noisily and a long, thin branch scratched against his bedroom window. *It'll be a tough day to play,* he thought, lying under his warm covers and looking at the soccer posters on his wall.

At breakfast, Tyler stared out the kitchen window. The trees swayed in the strong, gusting breezes. "What time is your game today?" his mother asked, putting a bowl of cereal at his place.

"Eleven o'clock," Tyler said, checking the schedule on the refrigerator for the tenth time.

"Dad's going to the neighborhood meeting at the library this morning," his mom said. "He'll try to make the second half of your game." She glanced out the window. "Maybe the wind will die down by then."

It didn't. As the Cougars waited for the Hornets to kick off a few hours later, the wind came at them full force. Their shirts and shorts flapped against their bodies like loose sails. The Hornets had the wind at their backs and started fast. They kept the ball at the Cougars end and forced Ramon to make a pair of tumbling saves.

Ramon and the Cougars tried to clear the ball, but the wind and the Hornets drove it back. Ben misjudged a high bounce and a Hornets forward swept in and pushed a low pass to the middle. Another Hornets player raced in and blasted the ball past the helpless Cougars goalie.

The Cougars were behind 1–0.

And the wind was still against them.

Coach Murray paced up and down the sidelines. "Come on, Cougars. Tough D. Keep the ball on the ground. Hang in there. Get the ball to Gavin and Mario."

Gavin was quickly becoming a key player for the Cougars. As the clock wound down for the first half, he made a mad dash along the right sideline, dribbling past two Hornets defenders. About 30 yards out from the goal, he sent a back pass to Tyler.

Tyler could see the play developing in his mind as the ball skidded toward him. He settled it with his left foot and instantly punched a pass up to Gavin, who was running free between two Hornet defenders in the middle of the field. The ball met Gavin just 15 yards from the goal. The fleet forward twisted his body and slammed a left-footed shot into the upper left corner of the goal. The Cougars were on the scoreboard!

The game was tied, 1–1.

"That's my man, Fast Freddy!" Tyler shouted, grabbing Gavin with one arm around his shoulder.

The wind swirled even more wildly in the second half, turning the game into a sloppy struggle in the middle of the field. Midway through the half, the Hornets goalie boomed a punt from his penalty area. Tyler drifted back to the spot where he thought it would land. He braced himself to head the ball. But just as he leaped to make the header, a gust of wind pushed the ball down. Instead of landing on Tyler's forehead, the ball bounced at his feet and hit him in the stomach. "Unnnnh!" he grunted.

A quick-thinking Hornet swept up the ball and raced downfield.

It's definitely a tough day for soccer, Tyler thought as he wheeled around to chase the play.

Minutes later, just as the game seemed to be drifting toward a tie, the Hornets attacked. A series of short, crisp passes brought the ball just outside the penalty box. Tyler slid in from behind, trying to knock the ball away from the Hornets forward. But just as Tyler's foot was about to meet the ball, the Hornets player passed to his left. Another Hornet spun a low shot from 15 yards out.

Ramon, the Cougars keeper, leapt to smother the ball. But the ball glanced off his lowered shoulder and bounced into the net.

The Cougars were behind, 2–1.

As the teams readied for the kickoff, Tyler saw three Cougars reserves running onto the field.

"Ty! Mario! Gavin!" they shouted.

Tyler jogged off the field, panting and desperate for something to drink. Coach Murray handed him a cup of water. He grabbed it so fast that half the water splashed out.

"I want you guys to get your breath back and I'll put you back in a couple of minutes," Coach Murray explained. "We need you fresh for the finish."

"How much time left?" Mario asked between gulps of water.

"I figure about six minutes," Coach Murray said, checking her watch. "But the ref keeps the official time."

The swirling wind swept along the Cougars sideline. Mario and Tyler kept their eyes on the game as they guzzled water and shook out their legs. Leading by a goal, the Hornets played keep-away to run out the final minutes on the clock.

"We gotta score," Mario muttered as he wiped sweat from his face.

"I know," Tyler said. He tossed his empty cup into the team's garbage box beside a pile of jackets.

"Subs!" Coach Murray shouted as the ball bounced out of bounds.

The referee blared her whistle and motioned to the Cougars bench.

"Ty, Mario, Gavin!" Coach Murray shouted. The three boys raced back onto the field. Cheers from the sidelines chased them as they ran.

"Come on, Cougars."

"Keep hustling."

"You can do it, Cougars!"

We've got to score! Tyler thought. The action, however, stayed stubbornly in the middle of the field. He could almost feel the seconds, and maybe the whole Cougars season, slipping away.

Then Mario stole a pass and moved past midfield. Trailing him, Tyler called, "Mario! Back pass."

Mario nudged a pass back and raced down

the right wing. Tyler dribbled around a defender and saw Mario nearing the goal. From 40 yards out, Tyler boomed a high kick, hoping Mario would chase it down.

The Hornets keeper edged out toward Mario.

But Tyler's kick was higher and harder than he had intended. Riding the wild wind, the ball curved toward the Hornets goal.

Surprised, the Hornets keeper started back, but he lost his balance and stumbled in front of the net. At the last moment he leaned back and reached up, trying desperately to snag the ball. But he was too short and too late. The ball bounced behind him and skipped into the goal.

Tyler's teammates mobbed him in the middle of the field. They slapped him on the head and back and shouted into wind.

"All right, Cougars!"

"Way to go, Tyler."

"Let's get another one!"

Tyler smiled as he caught Mario's eye. "It was a lucky goal," he insisted. "I was trying to pass it to you."

“Well, great pass,” Mario laughed. “We’ll take it!”

A minute later the referee blew her whistle and waved her arms above her head. The game was over. The Cougars and Hornets had tied, 2–2.

“We’re still alive,” Mario said as the teams shook hands and left the field.

“Yeah,” Tyler said, looking at the treetops still dancing in the wind. “But just barely.”

Chapter 9

The next afternoon the Cougars were back at Green Street Park, practicing hard. Tyler darted between two defenders and dribbled to his right. After a quick touch, he stopped and spun back to his left, leaving one defender sprawling. With the last defender racing along beside him, Tyler sent a low, left-footed shot toward the goal. He knew it was good as soon as he kicked it. Sure enough, the ball bounced between the two sweatshirts lying on the grass. Tyler raised his hands above his head.

"Goal!" he shouted.

"So what's that make it now?" Ben asked.

"Four to three," Tyler answered.

“Game’s to five, guys!”

The Cougars kept playing as the sun slipped down behind the houses near the park and a new gust of fall leaves fluttered to the ground. Tyler smiled as the ball bounced back and forth among his teammates. The Cougars’ passes were as crisp as the autumn air. He and Mario were getting used to their new positions. And the new players, especially Gavin, were fitting in great with the rest of the team. Still, Tyler couldn’t help wondering if it was already too late to save the season.

His thoughts were interrupted as a fifth goal by Josh ended the game. The rest of Tyler’s team started whooping and shouting. “Sweet move!” Tyler called.

But we’ll need a lot more sweet moves to make the County Cup, he told himself.

A few minutes later, Tyler and Mario headed home together. The streetlights had just come on and the boys took turns kicking the soccer ball as they made their way along the sidewalk.

“That was another good workout,” Tyler said.

"Yeah, everybody's getting a lot better," Mario agreed.

"Even us," Tyler laughed.

The conversation continued to bounce back and forth between the teammates as the ball bounced between their feet.

"Gavin's an amazing passer," Mario said. "He's so fast, too."

"And Ramon is a decent goalie, but he's slow in the field."

"That's why it's good he's a goalie," Tyler said.

Tyler paused under a streetlight and flicked the ball above his head. He tried to catch it on the back of his neck, but the ball bounced off his head and into the street.

Beeeeep! A car swerved to avoid the ball.

"Watch out!" Mario shouted.

Tyler waited for the next car to stop. He grabbed the ball from the street, waved at the driver, and tucked it under his arm. "I don't know how the real Freddy Adu does that trick," he said when he was back on the sidewalk.

"Maybe he doesn't practice in front of moving cars," Mario said.

Tyler smiled and tucked the ball safely under his arm as he and his friend started walking again.

"Hey, look," Mario said, pointing to the glow of lights above the high school field in the distance. "Think there's a game?"

"Let's check it out," Tyler said, and broke into a trot.

The Putty Hill Panthers were going through their practice paces. Tyler and Mario stood next to a parent who was watching on the sideline.

"Are these all the kids on the team?" Tyler asked. He had counted only ten players.

"No," the mother answered. "There are six more."

Mario looked around the field. "Where are they?" he asked.

"At a tryout for a district level team."

"Wow, they can just blow off practice like that?" Tyler was surprised. He'd heard the Panthers coach was pretty strict.

The mother smiled. "Don't worry. They'll be here for the game," she answered.

On the field, Zack looked up from a practice drill and waved at Tyler and Mario.

Mario waved back, and Tyler lifted his right hand slightly above his hip.

"You know Zack Bell?" the woman asked.

"We used to play with him," Mario explained.

"He's a strong player," she said. "He really helps the team."

Zack jogged over and said something to Coach Wexler. Tyler could see the coach looking across the field at Mario and him. Then the coach said something back to Zack and nodded.

Zack sprinted across the field.

"You guys want to play?" he called out as he approached. "We're gonna scrimmage."

"Cool," Mario said, pulling off his heavy, hooded sweatshirt.

But Tyler didn't feel like hanging around Zack and his new teammates. "Um, I don't know," he said. "I've got a lot of homework."

"Come on, it's just for twenty minutes," Zack said. "We're always missing some guys, and six against six is much better than five against five."

"Okay," Tyler said, putting his stuff down on the sideline. "Twenty minutes."

The Panthers coach handed out bright yellow mesh vests to half of the players. Zack and Mario were on one team. Tyler was on the other.

The coach was after the players from the moment the scrimmage started. "Head up, head up...pass across the field...hustle back...pass and move."

Right away, Tyler noticed that the Panthers scrimmage was about a half step quicker than the Cougars scrimmages. He had to pass the ball more quickly and hustle the whole time.

The Panthers were more physical, too. They jostled Tyler on what seemed to be every possession. But the coach hardly ever called a foul. He let the teams play on.

About halfway through the scrimmage, Tyler brought the ball under control at midfield with a quick touch. A defender moved in to tackle the ball. Tyler blasted by the defender, dribbling downfield and slipping a centering pass to a Panthers forward, who boomed a shot wide.

"Good play!" the Panthers coach shouted. "What's your name?"

"Ty. Tyler Davis!" Zack shouted before Tyler could answer. "He can play."

A small smile spread across Tyler's lips. He ran down the field even harder and faster.

The scrimmage ended without any goals. Most of the Panthers quickly picked up their stuff and left.

"So how'd you guys like being Panthers... for twenty minutes?" Zack asked, lingering on the edge of the field as Tyler and Mario collected their sweatshirts, ball, and sports bags.

"It was cool," Mario said. "You guys play pretty rough, though."

Tyler pulled his sweatshirt over his head. "It wasn't all that different from playing with the Cougars," he said in an even tone.

Across the field, Coach Wexler was stuffing soccer balls into a large brown canvas bag. "Hey, Zack, bring your friends over here," he called, waving.

The three boys walked across the field to him. "I'm Coach Wexler," he said, reaching out to shake their hands. "You boys looked pretty good out there. Who do you play for?"

"The Cougars," Tyler answered. "In the regular league."

"My old team," Zack added.

Coach Wexler nodded. Then he looked Tyler and Mario up and down, as if he were trying to guess their weights and heights. "How would you guys like to play for the Panthers?" he asked finally.

Tyler's head snapped back in surprise. "Really?" he said.

"We could be teammates again!" Zack said, punching Tyler's arm. "All right!"

"Well, we've had some pretty good luck with Cougars lately," Coach Wexler said, smiling at Zack. "And we may need more players if any of our guys go to the district level. How about it?"

"Cool," Mario said, sounding excited.

Tyler thought for a minute. If he left the Cougars for the Panthers, he'd be just like Zack. And what about Gavin, Chris, and the other Cougars? He couldn't leave them now, just when the team was starting to come together. *No,* Tyler told himself finally. *I want to win with the Cougars!*

Tyler shook his head. "No thanks, Coach. Mario and I are going to stay with the Cougars."

"We are?" Mario asked, frowning.

"Yeah, we've already started the season. It wouldn't be fair to leave the team now," Tyler said, eyeing Zack.

"Come on, Ty," Zack pleaded. "We could be on the same team again."

Coach Wexler held up his hand. "I understand," he said. "You guys are loyal to your team." He nodded toward Zack. "I had to ask your friend here a whole bunch of times before he came over to us." He slung the canvas bag over his shoulder. "I'll see you guys later," he said, walking away.

Zack studied Tyler. "Are you sure you don't want to play for the Panthers? It's pretty cool."

Tyler shook his head.

"Okay, well, you guys want a ride?" Zack asked. "My dad is pulling up."

"No thanks, we'll walk," Tyler said.

"Okay." Zack shrugged. "See you around, then. Thanks for playing." He raced to his father's car. Tyler and Mario returned to the winding sidewalk. They walked quickly, foot-tapping the ball back and forth between them. The streetlights seemed brighter and the night cooler as the evening grew darker.

"So you didn't want to play with Zack...even on the Panthers?" Mario asked.

"No way," Tyler said. "We have our team."

Mario sighed. "I guess you're right," he said. "It wouldn't have been fair to everybody on the Cougars if we just quit during the season."

Tyler nodded. "Yeah. But it was kind of cool that Coach Wexler asked." After a few more kicks, he added, "You know, they weren't *that* good."

"What?"

"The Panthers. They're a little quicker and play a little rougher. But they weren't so much better than our team."

"Maybe the missing kids were their best players," Mario pointed out.

"Maybe, but we can still play with those guys," Tyler said. "I mean, unless those missing guys are a *lot* better, we could give the Panthers a game in the County Cup."

Mario groaned. "Stop saying that. We're never going to play those guys in the County Cup—unless we start winning."

Tyler looked straight at Mario. "Then we'd better start winning."

Chapter 10

Tyler woke quickly and pulled on his uniform. He was wide awake and pumped: It was game day!

He hurried downstairs and grabbed some leftover pepperoni pizza from the refrigerator. His father was at the kitchen table, eating a bagel and looking at the screen on his laptop.

Tyler sat across from him.

"What are you eating?" his father said.

"Pizza," Tyler said, taking a bite.

"Cold?"

"Yeah, it's good," said Tyler as he chewed.

Tyler's dad rolled his eyes and looked back at his computer screen. "Zack's team won last night," he said, scrolling down.

"Listen to this: 'Zack Bell put the Panthers ahead to stay when he blasted a shot into the goal late in the first half.'" Then Tyler's dad looked up. "Have you seen Zack lately?"

"Mario and I practiced with his team this week," Tyler said as he got up to get some milk from the refrigerator. "They're good, but they're not *that* good. Coach Wexler even asked Mario and me if we wanted to join the team."

"Really? That's great. What did you tell him?"

"I said no, I wanted to stay with my team."

"I see. How does Zack like the team?" Mr. Davis asked.

"Okay, I guess," Tyler answered. He looked in the dishwasher for a glass. "Dad, is the stuff in here clean?"

"Yeah, we ran the dishwasher last night. So how are the kids on the team? Nice?"

"They're okay, but Zack says they really just get together for games."

"Doesn't seem like a real team, then."

"Yeah, that's what I think," Tyler said.

He poured the milk into a glass and sat back down at the table. “And I like being on the Cougars. I think we’re going to get a lot better.”

Tyler’s father closed his laptop. “Who are you guys playing today?” he asked.

“The Titans,” Tyler said. He gulped down the whole glass of milk and wiped his mouth with the back of his hand.

“Are they any good?”

“We pounded them 4–0 last year,” Tyler said. “But that was last year.”

“So how do you like playing midfield?”

“It’s good. I’m in the middle of all the action,” Tyler said, glancing at the clock. “We’d better get going,” he said. “Coach likes us there early.”

“Let me finish eating,” his father said, grabbing his bagel. “How are the new kids working out?”

“Great. Gavin’s super fast and he has some really smooth moves. And the other kids are getting better.”

“Well, you must be getting better, too,” his dad said. “You’re practicing almost every day.”

"I guess we'll find out today," Tyler said. "Come on, Dad. Let's go."

An hour later, Coach Murray gave the Cougars her final instructions. "Don't bunch up, guys. Let's try to get the ball to Tyler in the middle. Gavin, Mario, and Josh, give him somebody to pass to." She looked over the boys' heads to the referee blowing his whistle in the middle of the sun-drenched field. "Okay, Cougars, let's play hard and keep hustling."

The Cougars played hard, but couldn't make much happen. They started slowly with sloppy plays and passes. Near the end of the first half, Tyler sensed the team starting to pass better, pushing the play into the Titans' end of the field. The Titans boomed several long kicks out of their end just to relieve the pressure on their goalie.

One long kick sailed all the way down the field. New Cougars player Mikey Thomson, substituting at defense for Ben, got the ball. But instead of passing the ball up the side-lines, the Cougars rookie tried a long pass up to Tyler at center midfield.

"No!" Tyler shouted. But it was too late.

The Titans pounced. A midfielder intercepted the pass and dribbled into the heart of the Cougars defense. Chris charged forward to challenge the ball. But a Titan slipped a perfect pass to one of his forwards, who guided the ball into the unguarded side of the net for an easy goal.

Just like that, the Cougars were behind 1–0.

At halftime, Tyler barely heard Coach Murray. He sat on the sidelines, sucking on an orange and feeling as if his team's season was slipping away.

Like that old man Mr. Robertson had said, sometimes games were decided by one play. *And sometimes,* Tyler thought, *that one play goes against you.*

The Cougars started slowly again in the second half. The Titans seemed happy to protect their lead by falling back on defense and kicking the ball as far away from their goal as they could.

Then Tyler felt the team start moving again. It was almost as if the Cougars were playing one of their fast pickup games at

Green Street Park. Suddenly their passes clicked one step ahead of the Titans. Chris to Ben. To Tyler. Up to Josh. Back to Tyler. Over to Gavin. Soon, with Tyler directing play from midfield, the Cougars were buzzing around the Titans net.

Gavin beat a Titans defender to a loose ball. The speedy forward darted toward the middle and threaded a low pass across the mouth of the goal. Quick-thinking Mario stretched out his foot and angled the ball into the net.

Now the score was tied, 1–1.

All right! Tyler thought.

But the team didn't slow down to celebrate. The Cougars kept the pressure on. Gavin blistered a long shot that sailed by the diving Titans goalkeeper, ricocheted off the post, and bounced wildly in front of the net.

Seeing the play in front of him, Tyler darted past two Titans defenders and blasted the ball into the back of the net.

The Cougars led 2–1.

Tyler and his teammates didn't let up.

They were having too much fun. They jumped just a little higher than the Titans for every head ball, and every Cougars pass seemed to land at another teammate's foot.

Tyler watched confidently from the middle of the field as Mario launched a perfect crossing pass to the front of the goal. Gavin soared above two Titans and hammered a header past the goalkeeper for the final goal.

The Cougars won, 3–1!

Tyler grinned from ear to ear as he walked off the field with Mario. No one could stop talking about the game. "Wow. We really had it going today," Tyler said. "Josh, Ben, Chris...the whole team played great."

"You were awesome at midfield," Mario said, punching Tyler's shoulder. "I'm telling you, you're the new Z-man."

"Hey, what about you?" Tyler laughed. "First you had that great goal. And your crossing pass to Gavin at the end was dead-on."

"Yeah." Mario grinned. "Our Fast Freddy is a born goal scorer."

Tyler nodded. The Cougars—and their season—were finally starting to come together. The forwards were better than ever. Their defense looked solid with Ramon in goal and Chris at sweeper. And he was feeling great now at midfield.

Saturdays were going to be a lot more fun from now on.

Chapter 11

Tyler and Mario scrambled up the stairs of the Davis house. "Keep it down, Ty," his father called from the upstairs office. "I'm trying to get some work done."

Tyler poked his head into the room. "Me and Mario are going to hang out in my room for a while," he said.

"Mario and I," Mr. Davis corrected.

"Mario and I," Tyler repeated.

"How was school?"

"Fine."

Tyler and Mario threw open the door to Tyler's room and tossed their backpacks on his unmade bed.

"How much time before the team is getting together at the park?" Mario asked.

"I told everybody three thirty. So we've got to leave here in a half hour."

"Cool."

Mario grabbed the Cougars season schedule off the desk, dropped into the swivel chair, and propped his feet up on the edge of Tyler's bed.

COUGARS SCHEDULE

September 4	Tazmaniacs	L 1-0	2 p.m.
September 11	Hornets	T 2-2	11 a.m.
September 18	Titans	W 3-1	10 a.m.
September 25	Predators	W 3-0	3 p.m.
October 2	Strikers	W 2-1	Noon
October 9	Mud Dogs	T 1-1	2 p.m.
October 16	Knights	W 4-2	10 a.m.
October 23	Leopards	W 2-1	1 p.m.
October 30	Mustangs		2 p.m.
November 6	County Cup Tournament		

"Five wins, a loss, and two ties," he said finally. "That's better than I ever thought we'd do."

Tyler nodded. "Gavin turned out to be awesome," he said. "And the other guys improved a lot because of all our practices."

"Do we still have a chance to make the tournament?"

"I think so, but let's check." Tyler stood at his computer and tapped on the keyboard.

TEAM	Wins	Loss	Ties	Points*
Mustangs	6	1	1	19
Cougars	5	1	2	17
Hornets	5	2	1	16
Tazmaniacs	4	2	2	14
Mud Dogs	4	2	2	14
Leopards	3	3	2	11
Strikers	2	3	3	9
Titans	2	5	1	7
Knights	1	6	1	3
Predators	0	7	1	1

* Win equals 3 points
Tie equals 1 point
Loss equals 0 points

"I hope Ramon's dad updated the league Web site," Tyler said. "Here it is."

Mario leaned closer to the screen. "Where are the standings?"

"Right here," Tyler said, pointing.

"So if we beat the Mustangs on Saturday," Tyler said, "we win the league. If we lose or tie, they win. It's pretty simple."

"We would have won the league easy if we still had Zack, Justin, and Nate," Mario said. He grabbed a soccer ball from the floor and spun it in his hands.

"We did fine without them," Tyler said firmly. "And anyway, it's better without Zack. The games are closer, so they're more exciting. And more kids get a chance to play."

"Yeah." Mario looked at the standings again. "Hey, who beat the Mustangs, anyway?"

"I think it was the Mud Dogs."

"What? They're not that good."

"Let's check it out," Tyler said, clicking away. "Mr. Campos does a write-up of every game. Here it is: the Mud Dogs versus the Mustangs."

He read the write-up aloud:

The Mud Dogs upset the previously undefeated Mustangs in a hard-fought game, 1–0. Bobby Wilden scored the only goal of the game early in the second half when he converted a loose ball rebound in front of the Mustangs net. According to Coach Steve Tufano, the Mustangs were missing four key players due to a band concert at Roosevelt Middle School.

Tyler and Mario exchanged high fives. "Let's hear it for the Roosevelt Middle School band," Mario hooted.

"See, anything can happen in one soccer game," Tyler said. "And in one play."

"Yeah," Mario said, still laughing. "Especially if half of the other team is off blowing horns in a school concert."

He suddenly stopped laughing and sat up straighter. "Hey, where's that book you were telling me about in school? The one about the famous World Cup game that

English guy at the Panthers game was talking about."

Tyler flopped belly-down across his bed and reached under it. He pulled out a broken stopwatch, an old school permission form, and a pair of dusty underwear. Finally he pulled out an equally dusty book. "Got it," he said.

"It looks kind of old," Mario said. He sat up on the bed, peering over Tyler's shoulder as Tyler flipped through the pages of the *Spalding Soccer Handbook.*

"Yeah, but it's still got lots of cool stuff about the World Cup."

The two boys studied the book as if it were a map to buried treasure. "Here's the stuff about that 1950 England–United States game that Mr. Robertson told us about," Tyler said. "Look, here's an old newspaper story. Listen."

The United States today defeated England 1–0 to add the latest and biggest upset in the World Soccer Championships. The favored

British team and the spectators were stunned by the result. The lone tally of the match was scored by Joe Gaetjens at 39 minutes of the first half.

Brazilian fans swarmed onto the field after the United States victory and took the Americans on their shoulders while the victors were given an ovation.

"Why were the Brazilian fans so excited?" Mario asked.

"Because England lost," Tyler said as he began to read from another part of the handbook.

The Brazilian fans, who had cheered for the Americans because England was considered one of Brazil's primary challengers for the championship, went wild. They lit firecrackers, set fire to newspapers, and jumped the moat surrounding the field to hug and carry off the stunned Americans.

"Pretty funny," Mario said. "Look, one newspaper reporter called it 'The Biggest

Shock in the History of International Football'!"

"Yep," Tyler said, snapping the book shut. "Anything can happen in one game."

Mario nodded. "I definitely think we can beat the Mustangs on Saturday." He checked the time on Tyler's computer. "Hey, we'd better get going to practice."

Mario moved toward the door, but Tyler stayed on the edge of the bed for a minute, staring at the cover of the old book. He thought about the ragtag group of American players who had beaten the best team of professionals in the world.

Maybe the Cougars *could* beat the Mustangs on Saturday. And maybe, just maybe, they'd get a chance to beat Zack and the Panthers, too.

Chapter 12

Tyler, Mario, and Ramon stood at the edge of the field, stretching. The Cougars game was next. A bright sun hovered above, but the day was cool, with a whisper of winter in the air. "How much time left in this game?" Tyler asked.

"I don't know," Mario said. "Can't be much longer."

"The Mud Dogs don't look so great," Ramon said.

The referee blew his whistle and crossed his hands above his head. The Mud Dogs celebrated. Their opponents slumped.

"Well, they must be pretty good," Tyler pointed out. "They're the only ones who beat the Mustangs, and they just won this game."

The Cougars ran onto the field and started practicing centering passes. "Looks like we're going to have a crowd for this one," Mario said to Tyler as they waited in the passing line and glanced around the field.

"Hey, if we win this game, we're number one in the standings," Tyler said. "I'd watch, too, if I wasn't playing."

"Come on, Cougars!" a couple of familiar voices shouted from the sidelines.

Tyler looked up from the pregame warm-up and saw Zack and Devante standing together on the sideline.

"Don't you have a game today?" Tyler called to Zack.

"Tonight," Zack answered. Then he added, "I figured I'd scout you guys in case the Panthers have to play you in the County Cup."

"Maybe you will," Tyler said. He finished the warm-up drill and trotted to the sidelines.

"Hey, what are you doing here, Devante?" he asked. "I thought you only liked football."

"I can probably stand watching one soccer game if you guys are in it." Devante grinned, then flipped a thumb toward Zack. "He told me this is a big game."

Coach Murray called the team together and got right to the point. "Okay, Cougars, we've got to win today. A tie won't do us any good," she went on, speaking a little faster than usual. "So we have to be aggressive. Take some chances."

She looked around at the team. "Gavin, use your speed to get to the goal. Tyler, push the ball up every chance you get and keep the pressure on. Ramon, if you make a save, get rid of the ball fast. Okay, guys. Hustle on a count of three."

All the Cougars in the circle stacked their hands.

"One...two...three...hustle!" they shouted.

The game started slowly. The Mustangs seemed happy just to pass the ball and look for an opening. The Cougars chased the ball and the game, but soon grew frustrated. *It's like they're playing keep-away,* Tyler thought, running up and down the field.

Late in the first half, the usually dependable Ben misplayed a ball. A Mustangs forward sprinted up the right sideline. Chris, the Cougars sweeper, rushed to meet the Mustang and the ball.

Sensing danger, Tyler dashed down the middle of the field to help on defense. The Mustangs forward sent a centering pass past Chris to a teammate near the goal.

At the last moment, Tyler frantically picked up speed to intercept the pass. He reached the ball just in time to toe-tip it away from the ready Mustang and right to the Cougars goalkeeper. Ramon scooped the ball up with both hands and flung a quick pass down the opposite sideline.

Mario boomed a long kick out of danger and into midfield.

Whoa, that was close, Tyler thought as he turned and raced downfield. *One play,* he reminded himself. *And it better be ours.*

At the halftime whistle, the Cougars flopped onto the sideline grass, breathing hard and fast. Tyler draped a heavy sweatshirt across his shoulders to fight off the autumn chill.

"We've got to keep the pressure on," Coach Murray said, pacing. "Remember, a tie and a loss are the same thing today. We've got to go for the win."

As the team ran on to the field, Tyler shouted, "Come on, Cougars! We just need one great play!"

The second half was a replay of the first. The Mustangs played it cool, barely trying to score a goal. Their midfielders dropped back on defense, trying to control play and clog the middle of the field. A tie game was fine with them. They'd be league champs with either a win or a tie.

Tyler could sense the Cougars' chances fading as the clock ticked away. He noticed the referee glancing at his watch. The Mustangs had the ball. Tyler angled in toward the Mustangs midfielder and tried a slide tackle to knock the ball loose.

Tweeeeeet! The referee blew his whistle and signaled a Mustangs free kick.

"Come on!" Tyler protested, scrambling to his feet and flinging his arms out wide in frustration.

Moments later, Tyler intercepted a pass at midfield. He passed to Mario, who booted a long kick into the Mustangs zone. Gavin sprinted upfield to battle a Mustangs defender for the ball. The speedy sixth-grader tipped the ball free, spun past two defenders, and dribbled toward the goal.

A Mustangs midfielder dashed back and knocked the ball away from Gavin with an expert slide tackle. The ball trickled past the end line.

Tweeeeeet!

The referee pointed to the corner of the field, then checked his watch.

"Corner kick!" Coach Murray shouted, moving up the sidelines and waving her arms to get the Cougars to set up quickly.

"I got it!" Tyler yelled, racing toward the corner. He placed the ball in the quarter moon area marked near the corner flag and stepped several paces back. He glanced toward the goal.

The Cougars and Mustangs jockeyed for position in front of the net. The Mustangs goalie tried to direct traffic with his shouts and his gloved hands. "Get number nine. Watch out for the far post. Who's got that fast kid?"

Tyler stood at the corner and took a deep breath. *Make sure to hit it high and long enough to give Mario or Gavin a chance to make a play,* he reminded himself as he stepped forward.

Wham! Tyler's foot felt good on the ball and he smiled as it sliced the air—plenty high, and long enough.

Mario moved quickly, crashing through players. He jumped, almost climbed, over a group of Mustangs defenders in a perfectly timed leap. From the corner, Tyler could hear the clean, hard thud of the ball against Mario's forehead. In a flash, the ball rocketed by the Mustangs surprised goalkeeper. The net sprang backward.

Goal! The Cougars were ahead, 1–0!

Tyler leaped into the air. Mario ran a few steps and fell to his knees. The Cougars fell on top of him in a pile.

The Mustangs stood around the goal, stunned.

The game started again. But by now the Mustangs were so used to holding back and trying to protect their 0–0 tie that they could hardly mount an attack. With just a few minutes remaining, the Cougars gleefully played keep-away and sent long kicks back into the Mustangs zone.

Tyler kept looking at the referee. "Come on, clock," he whispered under his breath as he chased the ball, "get ticking."

Finally the referee blew his whistle and crossed his hands over his head. The game was over. The Cougars had beaten the Mustangs, 1–0.

The Cougars were league champions... and they were in the County Cup!

Mario raced down the field, smiling and pumping his fist. Tyler met him at midfield. "We're number one!" he shouted.

Mario held up one finger above his head. "*One play!*" he shouted back.

Chapter 13

Tyler ran down the field as fast as he could, chasing Devante and the ball sailing through the autumn sky. Devante reached up, ripped the ball out of the air, tucked it under his arm, and sprinted away. Tyler trailed helplessly, then gave up as Devante ran past a small bush at the side of the park.

"Touchdown!" Devante shouted. He turned, laughing. "We're ahead 4–1. Losers walk."

Tyler trudged up the field, kicking the dry dirt along the way. Mario and Gavin waited at the other end.

"You want me to try to cover Devante?" Mario asked.

"No, I got him," Tyler snapped.

"Doesn't look like it," Gavin said. "He's killing us."

"Hey, man, it's tough," Tyler said. "Devante's been playing football all fall. He's pretty good."

"Let's get a touchdown," Mario said as his team spread out to receive the kickoff. "One big play and we'll be right back in it."

"You guys need someone to cover Devante?" a voice called from the sideline. Tyler turned and saw Zack straddling his bike. Zack swung his leg over and let the bike fall. He walked toward the game, ready to play. Tyler's shoulders slumped. *What's he doing here?* he thought. "That's okay," he said aloud. "We've got even teams."

"Really? Come on, I could be on your team," Zack said, still walking toward them. "Looks like you could use some help."

"You're right about that, Zack," Devante called, twirling the football in his hands.

"Don't you have soccer practice or something?" Tyler muttered.

"Not today," Zack said. "I got the day off. Just like you guys."

"Come on, let's take him," Mario said. He turned to Devante's team and shouted, "Our team's got Zack. Okay?"

"No problem," Devante called. "We'll beat you anyway."

"Over here, Zack," Mario said, waving him toward the group. "You're with us."

"No!" Tyler shouted. He could feel his neck getting hot.

Everyone stopped and stared at Tyler.

"But we can use him," Mario said.

"No," Tyler repeated. "I'll cover Devante."

Zack stopped a few yards away from the team. His eyes moved from boy to boy and then settled on Tyler. "Fine. I don't have to play," he said, turning back toward his bike.

"Why don't you want Zack to play, Tyler?" Gavin asked.

"Because *he* didn't want to play with *us,*" Tyler said.

"Is that still bugging you?" Mario said, sounding tired. "Will you give it a break, Ty?"

Zack wheeled around. "Come on, Ty. I just went to another team."

"Yeah, *after* the teams were set for the season. You should have said no to the Panthers," Tyler said, looking around the group. "Just like I did."

"Wait a second. The Panthers asked you to play with them?" Gavin asked.

"Yeah." Tyler nodded. "Me and Mario. But we said no, we wanted to stay with our team." He looked directly Zack. "That's what you should have done."

"Hey," Zack protested. "Mr. Wexler asked me to play for the Panthers lots of times and I always said no. I just got sick of saying no. That's all."

"That's all?" Tyler exploded. The angry feeling he had kept inside for so long burst out of him. "You thought we weren't good enough!" he said.

"I never said that," Zack protested.

"Hey, are you guys gonna play or what?" Devante called. "All this arguing is making me think I'm at my house."

"Listen, I don't care if I play touch football,"

Zack said. "But if you want me to say I'm sorry for leaving the Cougars, forget it. I've had a good year. I learned a lot. I got better—"

"I thought being teammates was important," Tyler shot back before Zack could finish.

"Hey, whoa," Mario broke in. "Being friends is important, too."

"Come on, are you guys taking Zack or what?" Devante insisted. "Let's play some football."

Tyler turned to Zack, then to Mario, and finally back to Zack. "Okay, okay," he said impatiently. "We'll take Zack. You guys kick off. Let's go."

The ball spiraled through the air, angling to Tyler's side of the field. Tyler caught the ball, tucked it under his right arm, and started upfield behind Zack and Mario. He was close enough to touch Zack's back with the outstretched fingertips of his left hand.

Mario knocked a would-be tackler away. Without a word, Zack blocked another tackler to the left. *Nice block,* Tyler thought, but didn't say it out loud. He darted right and sprinted another 20 yards before Devante slapped his back with two hands for a last-ditch "tackle."

"I know you like to run to the right," Zack told Tyler. "I was looking out for you."

"Yeah," said Tyler. "Um, thanks."

"Who's quarterback?" Zack asked as he stepped into the huddle.

"Gavin," Ben said.

"So, quarterback, make a play."

Gavin drew the play on Mario's sweat-shirt as he talked. "Zack, line up on the left. Tyler, you're on the right. Both of you go down five steps and then slant in and cross."

"Switch sides," Zack suggested. "So Tyler's running right."

"What about me?" Mario asked.

"You're hiking. On two."

The boys lined up across the line of scrimmage.

"I got Zack," Devante called.

"Hut one. Hut two."

Tyler bolted off the line, ran five steps, faked left, and then angled right toward the middle of the field. He and Zack crossed, almost brushing each other's shoulders. Gavin plunked the football right into his chest. Tyler ran a few quick steps before he was tagged.

The huddle was full of talk and high fives.

"All right. Nice pass."

"Second down."

"I'll hike this time," Tyler volunteered.

"We're moving," Mario said. "Finally."

A couple of plays later, Zack slipped past Devante. Gavin lofted a long pass toward the end zone.

Tyler watched from the other side of the field as Zack took a few quick final steps, turned, and reached as high as he could. He snagged the high-flying football one-handed and yanked it tight to his body as he tumbled onto the grass.

"Touchdown!"

"What a catch."

"Losers walk!" Tyler shouted to Devante with a smile.

"Yeah, yeah, we know," Devante muttered as he and his teammates walked down the field. "We've watched you do it plenty of times."

One-handed, Tyler thought to himself. *Zack is always a player.*

The game moved on. With Zack's help, Tyler's team got closer but could never pull ahead. The sun dipped low and the shadows grew longer across the field. White puffs of hot breath floated in the still evening.

After the game, Tyler, Mario, and Zack sat at the base of a tree, drinking bottles of water.

"We almost caught them," Zack said, pulling on a sweatshirt over his head. "Devante is pretty tough. I couldn't cover him."

"You did okay," Mario said. "We still make a pretty good team." He grabbed Zack and Tyler in a double headlock.

"Yeah," Tyler admitted, wriggling free.

"So, you guys won the league," Zack said, changing the subject to soccer.

"Yeah. We were 6–1–2," Tyler said, sitting a bit higher.

"You did pretty well without me, I guess."

"We still could have used you," Tyler said.

"Yeah, but then you wouldn't have played midfield," Zack pointed out. "You must have done all right there."

"He was a Zack Bell clone," Mario said before Tyler could speak.

"Maybe not that good, but I did okay," Tyler said. He jerked his thumb toward Mario. "I set up this guy a couple of times in front of the goal so even he couldn't miss the net."

Mario flicked out a playful punch that Tyler blocked easily.

"So are you guys gonna be in the County Cup?" Zack said, taking a long gulp of water.

"Yeah," Tyler nodded. "What about the Panthers?"

"We're in it, too," Zack said. "Eight teams are in. They're supposed to post the first-round matches on the website in the next day or so."

Zack finished his water and smiled at Tyler. "Maybe we'll play each other in the first round," he said.

"Maybe," Tyler answered.

Zack stood up. "Well, good playing with you guys today." He grabbed his bike, rode across the field, and was swallowed by the dark.

"See, it wasn't so bad playing with Zack," Mario said.

"I know," Tyler agreed. "Did you see that catch he made in the end zone? One-handed!"

"The Panthers will be pretty tough in the County Cup," Mario said as he and Tyler started home.

"Yeah, but I still hope we play them in the first round."

Mario grinned. "Better be careful what you hope for."

Chapter 14

Mr. Martin stood straight and tall in front of the class. He was a very serious teacher, especially when it came to American history. “Quickly log onto your computers, everyone,” he said.

Tyler and Mario were sharing a computer in the back row of the classroom. Mario punched in their password.

“Your assignment is to research the most important battle of the Civil War.” Mr. Martin paused for dramatic effect. “The Battle of Gettysburg.”

He looked around the room. “Remember, you may use books, websites, essays, articles…whatever information you can find on the battle. Any questions?”

“Can we print out what we find today?”

"Yes, but no more than ten pages, and make note of your sources."

"How much time do we have?"

"Thirty minutes for research and then for the rest of the class we'll compare what we found."

Tyler and Mario traded glances and smiled. They each knew what the other was thinking. "Think it will be up yet?" Mario whispered.

"Coach Murray said they would post it today," Tyler answered.

"Did you check this morning?"

Tyler nodded. "It wasn't there."

Mario looked at Mr. Martin, who was walking slowly from computer to computer. "Maybe we should get something about Gettysburg first," he said.

Tyler glanced at Mr. Martin, too. The teacher was just a few computers away. "Okay. Let's Google 'Civil War battles.'"

The boys pulled up a site on the Civil War and leaned toward the screen. Mr. Martin looked over their shoulders, studied the screen briefly, and then moved on.

"Okay, we've got a few minutes," Mario

whispered excitedly. “We’d better try now.” He minimized the Civil War site.

“I’ll keep a lookout for Mr. Martin,” Tyler said. “He’s way across the room.”

Mario kept tapping away. “Hey, it’s not coming up,” he said.

Tyler leaned toward the screen. “You misspelled ‘league’. Hurry up.”

Mario hit a few more keys and the website popped up: www.WoodsideLeague.com.

“Click on County Cup. Quick,” Tyler said.

“Here it is,” Mario said. He and Tyler bumped fists without taking their eyes off the screen.

There, like a giant spider, were the brackets showing matchups for the eight teams competing for the County Cup. Tyler was pumped. “Look!” he said.

“Sweet! We play the Panthers in the first round,” Tyler said. He and Mario banged fists again.

“Gentlemen, does this have anything to do with the Battle of Gettysburg?”

Tyler and Mario straightened up and looked back. Mr. Martin was standing right

behind them. "Um, no sir," Tyler replied. "We were just taking a quick break."

"No breaks, boys. You are here to learn about the Battle of Gettysburg. It's a lot more interesting than you think. Back to work."

"Yes sir," Tyler replied. But right now he couldn't think of anything more interesting than next Saturday's game.

Chapter 15

Tyler stretched on the sidelines and looked up into the bleachers at the high school field. A large crowd was settling noisily in the stands. A big, bright banner declaring "County Cup" and dotted with Woodside Pizza logos flapped in the breeze.

"Pretty cool," Mario said, coming up beside him.

Tyler grinned. "Welcome to the big leagues."

Mario reached over the white-lined sideline and smoothed his hand across the close-cut green grass. "Nice field," he said.

"The short grass will make the game faster," Tyler said, still stretching.

"That might be good for Fast Freddy," Mario said, nodding toward Gavin in a cluster of Cougars. "Hey, he's going to be playing against his brother today. That's gotta be weird for Justin."

"Well, we didn't ask Justin to leave the Cougars," Tyler said.

"Wait a minute," Mario said, "look who's here."

Tyler looked over his shoulder. "It's Mr. Robertson, that English guy from the Panthers game."

Wearing the same battered cap and tweed jacket, the old man moved slowly along the edge of the field.

"Hey, Mr. Robertson!" Tyler called from the grass. "Remember us?"

Mr. Robertson looked confused at first. Then his face brightened.

"I thought you boys said you weren't good enough to play the Panthers."

"We've been practicing," Tyler smiled.

"Good," Mr. Robertson answered with a nod. He took a couple of steps toward the stands, then turned back to the boys. "You can beat them," he said. "Remember, any team can beat another."

Coach Murray walked by, clapping her hands. "Come on, Cougars, the game starts in ten minutes. Let's huddle up near the bench in five."

"Let's get the team together right now," Tyler said to Mario as the coach walked away.

"What for?" Mario asked.

"Well, we practiced with the Panthers, remember?" Tyler said. "I want to tell the team a few things."

A minute later, Tyler stood surrounded by his teammates. "We can beat these guys," he told them, his voice rising above the noise of the crowd. "Don't let those fancy travel team uniforms scare you."

He pointed across the field to Zack's team. The Panthers were kicking the ball lazily back and forth. They were smiling and laughing. "Mario and I practiced with those guys. We can definitely keep up with them. But we've got to hustle the whole game. We've got to compete for every ball.

In a close game, one or two plays decide it all."

Tyler motioned the Cougars in, and they drew closer around him. He punched the air and the rest of the team raised their fists, too. "Let's make sure *we* make those big plays," Tyler said. "Hustle on three."

"One...two...three...hustle!" the Cougars shouted together. After Coach Murray's final instructions, they ran onto the field, pumped and ready to play.

The game was quick and rough, just like it had been when Tyler and Mario scrimmaged with the Panthers.

The Panthers took control right away. Their passes were smooth and on target. Tyler kept feeling like he was just a split second behind each play.

A few minutes into the first half, Zack slipped by Tyler with a quick move. Tyler turned and raced to catch up with him, but Zack put a perfect pass at the feet of the Panthers right wing, who lofted a pass into the Cougars penalty area.

A Panther headed the ball past a leaping

Ramon Campos in the goal. But the ball skidded off the crossbar and out of bounds. Coach Murray shouted from the sidelines as Ramon boomed a long kick into the midfield. "Think about defense, Tyler...not so far up...don't take too many chances."

Coach is right, Tyler thought as he raced up the field. He knew he had to be careful. Zack could turn a mistake into a goal in no time.

The Cougars midfielders hung back and packed the defensive zone. The Panthers swung the ball coolly from side to side, patiently prodding the Cougars defense for a weak spot.

Suddenly a centering pass swirled dangerously close to the net. Justin Sheridan, now the Panthers left wing, raced in to head the ball. But Ramon stormed toward the ball and punched it away just before Justin could put it in the net.

Tyler controlled the spinning ball. He charged past Zack and looked upfield.

Fast Freddy, he thought, spying Gavin. Tyler sent a long kick up the right sideline straight to Gavin, who took control of the ball and raced upfield. He blasted a hard shot from outside the penalty area that whizzed wide of the goal.

Coach Murray ran up the sideline, clapping her hands. "Good play, Ty. Long passes. Look for openings."

But the Cougars' booming kicks and long passes couldn't stop the Panthers from creating more scoring chances.

Luckily the Panthers shots either sailed wide or were stopped by the Cougars goalie. Tyler could feel the Panthers growing more frustrated with every missed opportunity. He was starting to believe the Cougars could win this game.

The Cougars battled for every loose ball and didn't back down when the play got a little rough. As the first half wound down, Tyler and Zack waited together for a throw-in.

"It's still 0–0," Tyler said to Zack as the two boys in front of them jockeyed for position.

Zack smiled. "We'll see how long that lasts," he said.

Less than a minute later, Chris, the Cougars sweeper, sent Tyler a long pass. Zack darted forward, tipped the ball, and quickly gained possession. He easily dodged Ben Rosen, the Cougars defender, and bore down on the goal. Tyler scrambled to help on defense. Chris stepped out to stop Zack's rush. Ramon tensed near the goal line, ready to make a save.

At the last instant, just before Tyler and Chris could catch him, Zack angled a low pass to the left. His teammate Justin was right there to get it. Justin dribbled around Ben, the Cougars' last defender, and slipped the ball into the net before Ramon could react.

"Goooooaaaaaaal!" Zack shouted, almost into Tyler's ear.

The Panthers leaped in the air. They were ahead 1–0.

The Cougars slumped. Tyler turned away from the goal, put his hands on his hips, and stared up at the steel gray sky. Sure enough, Zack had turned one mistake—a careless pass by Chris—into a Panthers goal.

As the game began again, a sick feeling rose in Tyler's throat. He was tired. His legs ached. But that wasn't the worst of it. He felt sick because he *knew*. He knew his team was behind by a goal. He knew this game would not be like the World Cup match between the United States and England so many years ago. He knew that, in this game, one play would not be enough for a Cougar win.

Chapter 16

Coach Murray tried to keep the team's spirits up at halftime as the Cougars guzzled down water and breathed hard between gulps.

"Hang in there, guys," she said. "Don't give up. We're just down by one."

Tyler took some deep breaths and bit into an orange slice. He looked around at his teammates sprawled out on the cold, hard ground and wondered how much energy they had left. He knew everyone was playing extra hard just to keep up with the Panthers.

The Cougars gathered in a circle, piling their right hands in the middle. "Let's look for a quick opening," the coach instructed.

"Stay alert and be aggressive. On three. One…two…three…"

"Hustle!" the Cougars shouted and ran out onto the field.

"Twenty-five minutes!" Tyler shouted to his teammates from midfield. "Let's give it everything we've got."

The Cougars started the second half with a lot of fire. They beat the Panthers to almost every ball. The Panthers seemed to be playing at half speed, almost taking it easy. *Maybe they think the game is over,* Tyler thought as he ran down the field.

About ten minutes into the second half, the ball bounced loose near midfield. Tyler pounced, beating Zack to the ball, and raced toward the goal. Zack ran behind, barely keeping up.

Tyler spied Gavin racing down the right side. *I've got to get the ball to him,* he thought. *Fast Freddy will make something happen.* He chipped the ball over the Panthers defense. Gavin got it in stride. Tyler kept sprinting toward the goal. He could hear Zack behind him, still trailing the play. The Panthers defense moved toward Gavin to cut off the attack. But Gavin angled a low, skidding pass toward the middle of the field.

Tyler saw the pass—and his chance. He knew Zack was just a couple of steps behind him, so he didn't bother to stop the pass and set up a shot. He timed his run carefully and blasted the ball in full stride with his right foot. The ball hooked toward the far side of the net. The Panthers goalie leaped, stretching out as far as he could. He got a piece of the ball with the tips of his gloves. But it was too late. The ball bounced into the net and nestled in the corner.

Goal! The score was tied 1–1!

Tyler raised his arms and looked around the field. The Cougars were shouting and pumping their fists into the air. Up in the bleachers the Cougars parents were jumping, cheering, and high-fiving each other. Mr. Robinson was in the middle of them, waving one finger high above his head.

With one play, the Cougars were back in the game!

Tyler saw Zack, too. He stood stone still with his mouth hanging open, as if he couldn't believe the Cougars had tied his team.

The Panthers huddled on the sidelines. Tyler heard the Panthers coach shouting above the crowd. "Come on, get in the game. You should be crushing these guys."

"Better get ready," Zack warned as he and Tyler ran up the field, matching each other stride for stride. "We're done fooling around with you guys."

"No problem," Tyler answered, sounding almost as cocky as Zack.

The Panthers stepped up the pressure after Tyler's goal, coming out faster than ever. They sent low passes and high crosses into the Cougars penalty area. The Cougars hung on. Ramon kept the game tied with a tumbling save off a low shot by Justin. The Cougars goalie and his teammates tried to stop the Panthers with long kicks to clear the zone. But the Panthers kept coming back.

Tyler could feel his team getting tired. Just at that moment, Ben stole the ball from a Panthers player and raced downfield. Another Panther slid and tackled him at midfield. Ben fell hard to the ground and stayed there as the ball skipped out of bounds.

The referee blew the whistle and Coach Murray ran out to see if Ben, still lying face to the ground, was all right.

Tyler got the Cougars together. "Take a knee," he ordered. The Cougars all knelt down in midfield. "Let's take a quick break."

On the sidelines the Panthers coach shouted at the referee. "Come on, get a substitute in the game. You can't let them rest."

In the circle the Cougars took deep, quick breaths. Tyler looked over at Ben. He was still face down. Coach Murray sent Mikey Thomson in and helped Ben off the field. Ben stood up, carefully stretching his neck and shoulders. The crowd cheered as he walked slowly with Coach Murray toward the Cougars bench.

"Just ten more minutes of hard playing," Tyler told the rest of the team, estimating the amount of time left in the game. "Just like the beginning of the second half."

He looked at Gavin. "How are you feeling, Fast Freddy?"

Gavin shrugged. "Okay, I guess. My legs feel good."

"I'll try to hit you with a long pass," Tyler said.

As Ben passed the Cougars huddle he gave Tyler a funny smile. When he reached the sidelines, he flashed his teammates a quick thumbs-up.

Tyler almost laughed. Sneaky Ben had gotten an extra timeout for the tired Cougars.

As the game started again, the Panthers put more pressure on the Cougars. Justin lofted a dangerous pass from the right wing toward the Cougars goal, but Mikey leaped high above a tangle of players and headed the ball away. The ball bounced wildly at the top of the penalty area. Tyler and Zack sprinted toward the ball.

I've got to get it before Zack does, Tyler thought. He sure didn't want Zack to have the ball in the middle of the field so close to the goal. Tyler's foot made contact with the ball just a split second before Zack's. The Panthers midfielder stretched for the ball but slipped.

With a couple of quick touches, Tyler got the ball away from Zack and the middle of the field. *Where's Fast Freddy?* Tyler thought. When he looked up, he saw Gavin sprinting down the right sideline. Tyler blasted a long pass with his right foot.

Gavin broke free of the Panthers defense and drove a hard shot toward the far corner of the goal. The Panthers goalie leaped and managed to graze the ball with his fingers. The ball slipped by the goalpost and past the end line.

"Corner kick," the referee shouted, signaling with both hands. Then he looked at his watch. Tyler knew that time was running out.

Tyler raced to the corner, but Mario waved him off.

"I'll take the corner kick," Mario said. "You go to the middle."

Tyler joined the cluster of players in front

of the Panthers goal. He kept moving, trying to find a spot where he might be able to get his head, knee, foot—anything—on the ball to send it into the net.

Mario lofted a high pass into the pack of players. It looked as if it was heading right toward Tyler!

As he jumped, Tyler could feel Zack beside him. But before Tyler could crane his neck to put his head on the ball, the Panthers goalie crashed into the crowd and sent the ball flying back with a double-fisted punch.

Tyler fell to his knees. He turned and saw the ball spinning away from the Panthers goal and penalty area.

Mikey, the Cougars' substitute defender, raced up and slammed the ball back toward the goal. From his knees, Tyler watched the ball curve sharply. It sailed over the players crowded in front of the goal and into the upper right corner of the net!

Tyler sprang to his feet and ran wildly toward Mikey.

The Cougars were up, 2–1!

The team mobbed Mikey. They pounded his back and chanted, "Mikey! Mikey! Mikey!" The Cougars reserve looked a little stunned. Zack stood away from the Cougars, shaking his head.

Tyler pulled away from the happy circle, raised his fists, and shouted at the sky. He knew he had just seen the one play that would win the game.

After the final whistle, the happy Cougars lined up to shake hands with the disappointed Panthers. Standing at the front of the Cougars line, Tyler saw Zack lingering at the tail end of the Panthers line. His head was down and he looked as if he wanted to be anywhere but there.

The teams filed by one another, trading quick hand slaps and muttering "Good game." Finally Tyler reached Zack. "Good game," he said as he slapped Zack's raised palm.

Zack nodded. "Good game," he said and moved to the next player. Then he looked back over his shoulder and added, "You're not too bad at midfield."

Chapter 17

Tyler blew on his hands to keep them warm. He looked around the huddle. "Mario, fake a down and out," he said, drawing the pattern on Mario's sweatshirt. "Then go long."

"Devante's covering me," Mario said. "So I probably won't be open."

Tyler nodded. "Chris, line up left, go down five steps, and cut right. Ben, you hike on three."

The boys lined up. Tyler eyed the defense. "Remember, you guys have to count five Mississippi so I can hear you," he said.

"Just hike the ball," Devante called.

"Ready...set...hut one. Hut two. Three...."

Ben spun the football back to Tyler.

"One Mississippi...two Mississippi..."

Mario sprinted straight out, then cut to the sideline.

"Three Mississippi...four Mississippi..."

Tyler faked a throw to Mario. Just then, Mario spun to his left and sprinted up the field.

"Five Mississippi!"

Devante fell for the fake and stepped in toward the sideline, but he recovered quickly and raced after Mario. Tyler let a long pass fly just as a defender crashed by Ben and knocked Tyler down.

Tyler propped himself up on his elbows to see Devante intercept the pass. Tyler sank back to the ground. "Arrrrgh!" he shouted at the sky.

"I told you I wouldn't be open," Mario reminded Tyler when the team gathered in the defensive huddle.

"I thought you had a step on him," Tyler said.

"I did, but not for long," Mario said.

"Need somebody to cover Devante... again?" someone called.

The boys looked up. Zack stood at the end of the field. “How about it?” he called.

Mario eyed Tyler. “We sure could use him,” he said.

“Yeah, come on,” Tyler called, waving Zack in. “We got Zack,” he told Devante’s team.

“No sweat,” Devante said. “But it’s still 4–2. We’re ahead. Game’s to five touchdowns. So if we score, game’s over.”

Zack ran into the huddle.

“You’ve got Devante,” Tyler said, pointing at Zack. “They throw to him all the time.”

“Remember,” Devante said to Tyler before the play, stretching out the word. “It’s five Mis…sis…sip…pi.”

“You didn’t count like that,” Tyler told him.

“Why don’t we count to five *Maine*?” Mario suggested. “That’s shorter.”

“Let’s just play,” Devante pleaded.

A pair of quick completions moved the ball halfway up the field.

“Come on, let’s stop them,” Tyler barked at his teammates in the huddle. “You still got Devante, Zack?”

"He hasn't caught any passes yet, has he?" Zack asked.

On the next play, Devante angled into the middle of the field and then cut sharply toward the left sideline. Zack stayed with him step for step. He leaped up with his left hand to try to swat the ball away just as it arrived. But the pass was perfect, missing Zack's fingertips by an inch and smacking into Devante's hands.

Zack tumbled onto the dirt and watched helplessly as Devante ran down the sideline for the winning touchdown. He looked across the field at Tyler and shrugged.

The game broke up quickly. Tyler, Mario, and Zack stood in the middle of the field with the cold wind swirling around them. The bare trees reached up to the blue black sky.

"Sorry," Zack said. "Guess I didn't help much."

"That's okay," Tyler said. "None of us could cover Devante either."

"Hey, I heard you guys didn't do so well in the tournament after you beat us," Zack said.

Tyler laughed. "You could say that."

"Yeah, we lost 4–0," Mario chimed in.

"Ouch," Zack said. "Well, you never should have beaten us. I still can't believe Mikey got that lucky goal."

Tyler smiled at the memory of the ball flying into the upper corner of the net. "Yeah," he agreed. "It was kind of like Joe Gaetjens."

"Who's that?"

"He was the guy who scored a U.S. goal to beat England in the World Cup in..." Mario began. He looked at Tyler. "I forgot what year. A long time ago."

"In 1950," Tyler said. "And it was probably the biggest upset in soccer history."

"Until you guys beat us last Saturday, you mean," Zack teased. "So what happened to the U.S. team after they beat England?"

"They lost, big time," Tyler said.

"Just like us," Mario said.

Zack pulled the hood of his sweatshirt over his head. "So do you guys want to play for the Panthers next year?" he asked, shuffling his feet from side to side to stay warm. "Coach Wexler told me after the game to ask you guys again if you wanted to switch."

"Really?" Tyler and Mario said at the same time.

Part of Tyler still thought it would be cool to play on the Panthers. But now that the season was over and after the Cougars' big win, he knew there was no way he would leave his team.

"Coach liked Gavin, too," Zack said. "He said you three guys played every ball."

"You never know which play will win the game," Tyler said, echoing Mr. Robertson.

Zack nodded. "Well, how about it? Do you guys want to play for the Panthers or not?"

"I don't know, Zack," Tyler said with a small smile. "I was going to ask whether *you* wanted to come back to the Cougars."

"Yeah, Zack," Mario teased. "After all, we did beat you guys."

"By one lucky play," Zack protested.

"That's all it takes," Tyler said, throwing an arm around his friend's shoulder. "One play."

The Real Story

The 1950 World Cup:
United States vs. England

United States–1
England–0

The 1950 soccer match between the United States and England was the biggest upset in World Cup history. The game was played in Brazil, and when people back in England heard the final score, they thought it was a mistake. They had expected England to crush the United States 10–0.

Soccer was not a very popular sport in the United States in 1950. It's hard to believe, but back then, soccer was played mostly by kids at private schools or immigrants who had learned the game back in their home countries. Few people in America knew or cared about their soccer team. About four hundred reporters traveled to Brazil to cover the World Cup, but only one of them was from the United States.

Most of the members of the 1950 United States World Cup team had other jobs and played soccer on the weekends to have fun and to pick up some extra money. Joe Gaetjens, who scored the game's only goal, was an accounting student and part-time dishwasher. Frank Borghi, the team's sure-handed goaltender, was a former minor league *baseball* player who drove a hearse for his family's funeral business.

No one had high expectations for the American team. In previous international matches, American teams, with many of the same players, had already been trounced by Italy (9–0), Norway (11–0), and Scotland (4–0).

The English team, on the other hand, was loaded with top players from the best teams in their country—stars from Manchester United, Arsenal, Blackpool, and Liverpool. The English team's record in international matches stood at 23–4–3.

The game against England started as if it would lead to still another American defeat. The English pros dominated play with short, crisp passes. The American amateurs tried hard just to keep up.

The English blasted six shots at the American goal in the first twelve minutes, including two that bounced off the goalposts. The United States team didn't manage its first, weak shot on the English goal until the twenty-five minute mark.

But the second American shot, twelve minutes later, changed everything. Walter Bahr, the team's captain, who would later coach the Penn State University soccer team, sent a hard, shoulder-high shot to the right of the English goal. The ball spun across the field, about 12 yards in front of the goal. The shot seemed harmless until the American center forward, Joe Gaetjens, dove flat out to head the ball. Teammate

Harry Keough later remembered that Gaetjens leaped "as though he thought he could fly or something." Gaetjens fell belly-first to the ground, but his head nicked the ball just enough to send it into the net!

At halftime the United States led 1–0, despite being outshot 14–2 during the first half. England continued to dominate play during the second half. But they still couldn't score. Some shots sailed wide of the net, but many were knocked away by Borghi, the American goalkeeper.

The Americans almost scored again on a header by Gaetjens. But as the game wore on, the Americans began to get tired. With eight minutes remaining, England's star forward, Stanley Mortensen, broke free and dashed toward the American goal with the ball dancing at his feet. Charley Columbo, the center halfback for the United States and the toughest player on a team of tough players, chased after Mortensen. Just outside the penalty area, Columbo dragged Mortensen down with a flying American football-style tackle. The play wasn't very fair, but it probably saved a goal.

On the free kick following the Columbo penalty, an English forward headed the ball toward the American goal. Borghi leaped backwards and slapped the sure score away just inches from the goal line.

The United States held on to win the game 1–0. Thirty thousand happy Brazilian soccer fans flooded the field and carried Gaetjens and Borghi away on their shoulders. The Brazilians were thrilled that someone had beaten one of their biggest rivals.

The United States team, however, could not keep up their World Cup magic. They played Chile two days later and lost 5–2. The next day they boarded planes for the long trip home. Their country barely knew of the team's big upset. There were no television or radio reports of the game.

But every one of the eleven players on the team knew. They knew that on one amazing day, they had beaten the finest soccer team in the world. The American team had bested the mighty English pros because they knew what Tyler and his teammates learned: In soccer, sometimes it takes just one play to win.

Acknowledgments

Much of the information about the 1950 World Cup game between the United States and England came from *The Game of Their Lives: The Untold Story of the World Cup's Biggest Upset* by Geoffrey Douglas. In addition, the quotes in Chapter 11 were taken from the *Spalding Soccer Handbook* by Paul Harris.

About the Author

Fred Bowen was a Little Leaguer who loved to read. Now he is the author of many action-packed books of sports fiction. He has also written a weekly sports column for kids in the *Washington Post* since 2000.

For thirteen years, Fred coached kids' baseball and basketball teams. Some of his stories spring directly from his coaching experience and his sports-happy childhood in Marblehead, Massachusetts.

Fred holds a degree in history from the University of Pennsylvania and a law degree from George Washington University. He was a lawyer for many years before retiring to become a full-time children's author. Bowen has been a guest author at schools and conferences across the country, as well as the Smithsonian Institute in Washington, D.C., and The Baseball Hall of Fame.

Fred lives in Silver Spring, Maryland, with his wife Peggy Jackson. Their son is a college baseball coach and their daughter is a college student.

For more information
check out the author's website at
www.fredbowen.com.

Hey, sports fans!

Don't miss all the action-packed books by Fred Bowen.
Check out www.SportsStorySeries.com for more info.

Soccer Team Upset

PB: $5.95 / 978-1-56145-495-2 / 1-56145-495-8

Tyler is angry when his team's star player leaves to join an elite travel team. Just as Tyler expected, the Cougars' season goes straight downhill. Can he make a difference before it's too late?

Touchdown Trouble

PB: $5.95 / 978-1-56145-497-6 / 1-56145-497-4

Thanks to a major play by Sam, the Cowboys beat their arch rivals to remain undefeated. But the celebration ends when Sam and his teammates make an unexpected discovery. Is their perfect season in jeopardy?

Dugout Rivals

PB: $5.95 / 978-1-56145-515-7 / 1-56145-515-6

Last year Jake was one of his team's best players. But this season it looks like a new kid is going to take Jake's place as team leader. Can Jake settle for second-best?

Hardcourt Comeback

PB: $5.95 / 978-1-56145-516-4 / 1-56145-516-4

Brett blew a key play in an important game. Now he feels like a loser for letting his teammates down—and he keeps making mistakes. How can Brett become a "winner" again?

Fred Bowen Sports Story series

All-Star Sports Story series

Want more?

All-Star Sports Story *Series*

T. J.'s Secret Pitch

PB: $5.95 / 978-1-56145-504-1 / 1-56145-504-0

T. J.'s pitches just don't pack the power they need to strike out the batters, but the story of 1940s baseball hero Rip Sewell and his legendary eephus pitch may help him find a solution.

The Golden Glove

PB: $5.95 / 978-1-56145-505-8 / 1-56145-505-9

Without his lucky glove, Jamie doesn't believe in his ability to lead his baseball team to victory. How will he learn that faith in oneself is the most important equipment for any game?

The Kid Coach

PB: $5.95 / 978-1-56145-506-5 / 1-56145-506-7

Scott and his teammates can't find an adult to coach their team, so they must find a leader among themselves.

Playoff Dreams

PB: $5.95 / 978-1-56145-507-2 / 1-56145-507-5

Brendan is one of the best players in the league, but no matter how hard he tries, he can't make his team win.

Winners Take All

PB: $5.95 / 978-1-56145-512-6 / 1-56145-512-1

Kyle makes a poor decision to cheat in a big game. Someone discovers the truth and threatens to reveal it. What can Kyle do now?

Want more?

All-Star Sports Story *Series*

Full Court Fever
PB: $5.95 / 978-1-56145-508-9 / 1-56145-508-3

The Falcons have the skill but not the height to win their games. Will the full-court zone press be the solution to their problem?

Off the Rim
PB: $5.95 / 978-1-56145-509-6 / 1-56145-509-1

Hoping to be more than a benchwarmer, Chris learns that defense is just as important as offense.

The Final Cut
PB: $5.95 / 978-1-56145-510-2 / 1-56145-510-5

Four friends realize that they may not all make the team and that the tryouts are a test—not only of their athletic skills, but of their friendship as well.

On the Line
PB: $5.95 / 978-1-56145-511-9 / 1-56145-511-3

Marcus is the highest scorer and the best rebounder, but he's not so great at free throws—until the school custodian helps him overcome his fear of failure.

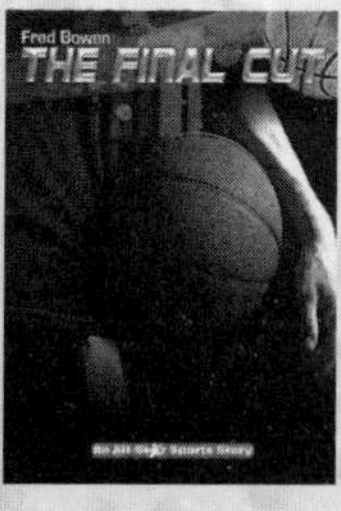

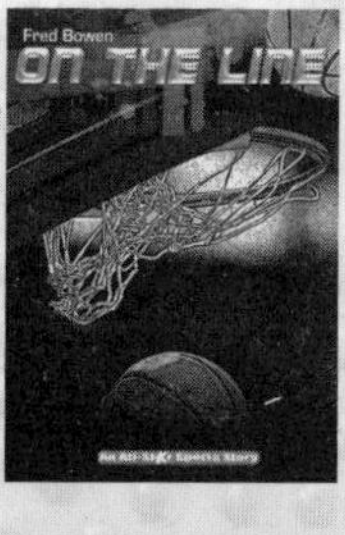

All-Star Sports Story series